Devil of Mine

A PREQUEL NOVELLA

MOST IMPRUDENT MATCHES

ALLY HUDSON

To all those who've loved and lost...

It's a sad song / It's a sad tale, it's a tragedy/ It's a sad song / But we sing it anyway

— ANAÏS MITCHELL, *HADESTOWN*

Devil of Mine

Introduction

Dearest Reader,

A (not so) brief content warning: This novella is set a decade before the events that occur in the rest of the series. If you've read any of the other books in the Most Imprudent Matches series, you already know Celine is a widow. This is the story of her first marriage.

Contained in the following pages is a story of love and of loss. There is an on-page depiction of the male main character's death. It is not a pleasant death.

I hesitate to call this novella a romance because, although you will read about love in this story, there is no happily ever after for Celine and Gabriel. Gabriel's story ends here.

Celine will get her happily ever after, but she will not be the same youthful, carefree Celine we meet today. After all, none of us will love with the same enthusiasm and recklessness at thirty as we did at twenty.

I've considered many ways of presenting this story to you. I debated cutting the last few chapters. I considered releasing it as a free e-book for my email subscribers. I've considered not releasing it at all. However, none of those options allowed me to tell Celine's story in the way I wanted to with the quality it deserved.

I completely understand why a reader might want to skip such a novella. So here is your warning. If you want to embark on the entirety of Celine's journey, it starts here. If you'd like to experience this story but end on a happy note, you can stop reading when you finish chapter 19. If you'd rather experience only Celine's happily ever after, you should skip to book four, *Angel of Mine*.

All of my books are written to stand on their own. You will not have difficulty understanding future books no matter what you choose.

If you have decided to continue on, I invite you to fall in love with Gabriel Hasket, Marquis of Rycliffe.

Thank you and happy reading,

Ally

One

HASKET HOUSE, LONDON - AUGUST 22, 1806

THIS ONE WAS PARTICULARLY DULL. They all were, of course, but this one especially. Viscount Lucas? Baron Lucas? He was pompous enough to be titled, certainly.

He was handsome—in the right light and after a few glasses of sherry. Neither lighting nor sherry could make him less tedious though.

"Noble Blossom Kramer is the sire, of course, but..." the lord droned on. Good lord, surely he was not intending to detail the pedigree of every single horse in his stables. And, honestly, what sort of name was Noble Blossom Kramer? Why could he not have been one of the dazzled ones? *They* usually afforded me the courtesy of awestruck silence.

"His breeding is so excellent, I expect, after he leaves the starting gate, he'll stop to close it behind him!" he said with a conspiratorial jeer.

Was that intended to be a joke? I offered a feminine giggle and it seemed to placate him. It also set him to talking about the other twenty-eight horses he owned.

Absolutely not.

Since Lord Lucas had no intention of retreating on his own, I would need to organize my own rescue.

With the kind of casualness that could only be feigned, I dragged a delicate finger across the swell of my breasts, brushing away an imaginary irritant. *There it is...* the dazed silence.

The blessed relief lasted only a second before he recalled his horses—this time directing his comments to my bosom. Suitor distracted for the foreseeable future, I swept an appraising gaze across the ballroom.

Baron James—too old and repugnant. The Earl of Westfield—equally elderly and more repugnant, if that was possible. Also married. Truly, the selection was abysmal.

I had higher hopes for one of Her Grace's fetes.

That was unkind, the Duchess of Rosehill knew how to host a ball, even if a slightly garish one. It was the gentlemen who were not doing their part. Entirely uninspiring, the lot of them.

Mr. Parker—certainly not. Although he was an entirely appropriate age, unwed, and passably handsome, he never spoke except to insult someone. A wallflower, a sixth son, a servant—he wasn't particular about his victims.

I released a distracted sigh. Lucas faltered for a moment, struck by my décolleté again.

My gaze caught on Mr. Ellsworth. He would have to do for now. Untitled and in possession of a not-particularly-noteworthy pocketbook, he was the least pitiful to look upon and was, on occasion, amusing.

It was the work of a moment to catch his gaze from across the room. I glanced down before seeking his eyes again from beneath lowered lashes.

That did it.

He was halfway across the ballroom, and I didn't even

need to offer him the shy smile. And never mind my fan, which hung untouched from its strap on my wrist.

It was the lack of title—it made him overeager.

"And Xerxes Stormfeet was foaled last M— Oh!"

Ellsworth clapped Lucas on the shoulder, finally ripping his gaze from my bosom. I would need to use more consideration before employing that distraction in the future.

"Lucas, my good man, I just saw your sister heading to the orangery. She was arm in arm with one of the footmen," Ellsworth said. He had the good sense to keep his voice low; at least he wouldn't ruin some poor girl in his rescue attempt. I hadn't even known Lucas had a sister. Or that Her Grace had an orangery...

Lucas hesitated, glancing between Ellsworth and myself.

Filling my voice with concern, I added, "*Oh non!* I will save our dance for the next ball, my lord. You must see to her!"

For a moment, I worried he would actually leave his sister to ruin. I'd gone too far sprinkling in my mother tongue. The accent was too enticing for him.

The *beau monde* loved it. Never mind that I hadn't set foot in France since I was a child, not since Mama and I fled La Terreur. My accent—feigned more often than not—was enough to delight the simpletons of the *ton*.

After a moment of staring, dazzled and silent at last, he excused himself, no match for my expectant, concerned expression. With a bow, he wandered off looking lost.

"I had not thought there was an orangery," I commented to Ellsworth once Lucas was out of earshot.

"No idea. I wasn't even certain he had a sister," he shot back with a pleased grin.

The laugh I gave him was genuine. The playful tap on his arm with my fan was less so. But he deserved a reward for such an efficient and successful rescue.

"You, monsieur, are trouble!"

His chest puffed out appreciatively in response to the compliment.

"Tell me, how is your family? Are they well?" I asked, determined to keep the conversation away from stables.

"My father's gout is acting up again. He..." *Oh, good lord.* Not one of these men had even a little sense.

That was when I felt it. Again.

That prickling tingle on the back of my neck, that *awareness* I hadn't sensed in months.

Someone was watching me.

Desperate to find the source, I made no effort to distract Ellsworth from my disinterest, turning my head wildly.

Nothing.

"Mademoiselle Cadieux?" Ellsworth asked, mangling the address.

Forcing my attention back to him, I replied, "Apologies. I thought I heard someone calling me. I must have been mistaken." The tingling awareness still dragged down my spine. "Perhaps it is the heat. It is quite warm in here. Is it not?" I asked.

The eyes, somewhere in this crowd, burned a path down my form. I was accustomed to attention, stares even. I rarely noticed. But thrice now that awareness had set fire to my skin. The Cavendish party, perhaps half a year ago, was the first time. Then at the opera two months ago, I felt it again. And now in the Rosehill ballroom...

"Shall I fetch you a lemonade?"

"That would be most appreciated, *monsieur*. You are my hero!"

Task in hand, he finally set off with purpose in his stride. I would need to be more careful with him. He would drop to one knee in two days if I gave him any further encouragement.

"And what did that one do to displease you?" A honeyed, masculine voice whispered low in my ear.

I whirled around with a gasp, only to meet with a broad, well-dressed chest, far too close for propriety.

As I tipped my head back, he chuckled. It was an amused, graveled sound. Back, back, and back. *Oh my...*

The crooked, closed-mouthed smirk was the first thing to catch my gaze. Then the teasing, ochre eyes. Near black hair, tousled, unkempt, and a touch too long, covered a too-prominent brow. The nose was askew, perhaps broken once.

This amalgamation, this *man*, shouldn't have been attractive. He was, however, easily the handsomest man in the room.

And that feeling, that niggling awareness, the fluttering in my chest, the twisting in my belly were all back, stronger than ever.

"Well?"

"I beg your pardon?" I asked, still starting wide-eyed and open-mouthed. It was possibly the least attractive expression my face had ever made.

"The nitwit you just dismissed. Is he so forgettable?"

I was wrong, his voice wasn't honey. It was the smoothest, richest bourbon, warming me from the inside out.

The sound was so intoxicating it took me a moment to parse out his meaning. He had noticed my little game. No one had ever noticed. Or they certainly hadn't been bold enough to comment on it if they did. Irritation twisted, warring with the fluttery warmth for prominence in my gut.

"I have no idea what you mean," I spat. My voice was too high, tinny, and filled with more desperate uncertainty and less sensual confidence than usual.

"You were holding court again." His smirk deepened. His upper lip was thin but the lower was full, and rose pink and impossibly soft looking.

"Excuse me?"

Was this how gentlemen felt in my presence? Distracted and fluttery and three steps behind?

"You're generally a much better liar than this." He frowned.

The accusation shot me back to the present. "You forget yourself, sir," I reprimanded.

His grin returned. A flash of straight, white teeth peeked from the uplifted corner, accompanied by a warm chuckle.

He was still too close and too hot. The heat of him burned from head to toe, thrilling along with the vibrations from his chuckle.

With a glance over my head, he grabbed my upper arm in his massive hand and hauled me to the dance floor where the first tentative strains of a waltz began.

I was small, but not notably so, and his hand covered the whole of my upper arm. How did such a large man move with such grace? Without a word, he manhandled me into position, looming into my space.

Of all the ungentlemanly, boorish behavior—

"Relax," he murmured in his silky baritone.

"Relax? You just accosted me in a ballroom." Far from silken, my speech was louder than I intended and bordering on shrill. I took a calming breath only to be enveloped with the spicy, citrus scent of bergamot—him.

"Hardly. Unless you were planning to continue manipulating the twit with the lemonade. He's still over there, looking forlorn. I could return you to him. If you'd like." He tipped his head to the edge of the dance floor. Ellsworth stood there, glass in each hand, looking like a lost puppy.

I should demand this man return me to my erstwhile suitor. I knew that.

But *this* man... He was certainly not dull.

If only I could focus, bring him to heel. Surely it was only the element of surprise that was affecting me this way, nothing more. It had nothing to do with the firm press of his hands encircling my waist as he guided me about the room so easily my feet barely felt the floor.

Swallowing my indignation, I worked my lips into the pout men found particularly alluring. Then I pressed my shoulders back, emphasizing the cut of my gown under the guise of posture. Finally, I glanced up to meet charcoal eyes, widening my own enticingly.

His grin shifted into something wry and amused. "That usually gets you what you want. Doesn't it? It won't work on me."

Instinctively, I sought to deny, feign ignorance. But... such efforts had proven ineffective against this man.

With a resigned sigh, my shoulders slipped down to resting. "What exactly do you want?" I asked.

"The same thing you do," he breathed low between us.

"And what is it that you think I want?"

His lip curled up before the word slipped out. "Entertainment."

"Entertainment?"

"You're disenchanted with the *ton*. I am as well. And you, Mademoiselle Cadieux, are the most interesting person I've seen at one of these events in a long, long time."

Soothed pride dampened some of the irritation heating my chest. "How do you know my name?"

"Everyone knows your name. The little French debutante charming the wits out of the entire *ton*."

"And your name?" I asked, struggling to hide my interest as the music came to a close. The final dirges of the tune echoed between us. I couldn't—didn't want to—break away to applaud the musicians.

He made the choice for me, hands slipping from my waist, leaving a seared brand behind. "Our dance is finished. Next time, perhaps."

He stepped back once, twice, dragging his gaze up and

down my form, setting fire to any doubt I had that his eyes were the ones responsible for that prickling, tingling awareness. There was no subtlety in his look and enough heat to burn the room to the ground.

Finally, he spun on one foot and strode off into the crowd, melting away.

My weight shifted to my toes without permission. But it was useless, I could see nothing over the sea of people crashing into me in his wake. He was lost entirely.

Dimly, I became aware of more than one curious onlooker —though certainly not the one I wanted. A group of ladies eyed me, whispering behind their hands. The gentlemen off to the side were less subtle in their appraisal.

Ellsworth found his way to me, warm lemonade still in hand. I paid him little mind, still scanning the crowd for a dark head.

"Are you all right, mademoiselle?" He asked from my side.

"Yes, of course. Why should I not be?" I was vaguely cognizant of Ellsworth's head flitting between me and the crowd.

"You seem distressed. Did he hurt you?" Ellsworth was undeterred by my disinterest. The mysterious gentleman was long gone. I bit back a sigh before turning to the inferior specimen at my side.

"*Oui, non.* I am perfectly well, but I thank you for your concern," I said. "And the lemonade."

A part of me wanted to ask for the man's name. It would be the work of a moment and a doe-eyed glance.

But for the first time in months, perhaps years, I wasn't bored. So I didn't ask. Because he had been right. A part of me —not one I was particularly proud of—wanted to play this man's game.

I wanted to be entertained.

Two

CADIEUX HOUSE, LONDON - AUGUST 23, 1806

THE EFFECT of my *je ne sais quoi* was somewhat dampened for the rest of the evening. Whether that was his doing—the mysterious gentleman—or my own vexed mood was entirely unclear. All that was certain was that the tingling, sparkling sensation setting my spine alight never materialized again.

He was gone to wherever it was that mysterious gentlemen disappeared.

But that was hardly relevant when I didn't have to summon a replacement to rid myself of Ellsworth. Desperate booby, Ellsworth...

Mama, seeming to sense my distress, had kindly feigned a megrim, though her motives may not have been entirely altruistic. She ended the evening looking rather more harassed than she had when we arrived. Her Grace had a tendency toward theatrics, and Mama was often called to soothe her nerves.

I slept fitfully that night, haunted by an infuriating smirk and mirth-filled umber eyes.

Still, I awoke to the usual collection of sundries waiting for me. The cream-and-sage drawing room of the house Mama and I had let just off St. James's square on King Street contained more flowers than most hot houses. The usual assortment of roses and carnations in reds, pinks, and whites lined every surface and spilled into the entry.

Perhaps the slow end of the evening was all in my mind. Perhaps nothing was truly amiss. There were cards from Ellsworth, Lucas, and Parker, and all the rest.

My lady's maid flitted into the room holding one last arrangement. Half a dozen royal irises rose from a thin silver vase. The metal was polished to such a gleam that my wide, surprised eyes stared back at me.

"Jane, was there a card with these?"

"No, mademoiselle, just the arrangement."

There were any number of explanations. Perhaps the card blew away during delivery. Perhaps it was mistakenly placed in another arrangement at the florist's.

But somehow, without a doubt, I knew. It was him. This arrangement was far too interesting.

"These in my room, if you please, Jane."

"Of course," she answered with an intrigued brow.

I had never, not once, requested she place an arrangement in my rooms. The flowers and gifts I received all remained here in the drawing room. Quite frankly, after three seasons, the ostentatious displays of roses and carnations were rather dull. Best to confine them to a singular room.

Also, callers enjoyed seeing their arrangement displayed prominently. If I had Jane switch out the arrangements on the mantle between gentlemen, they were none the wiser.

There would, however, be no caller attached to the irises. I was certain of it. And so, they could add interest to my boudoir.

The parade of suitors was even more tedious than usual this morning. The next man to recite Byron to me would get a shoe thrown at his head.

My irritation was new. Usually, I found the entire display some combination of flattering, amusing, and tedious depending on the suitor and the amount of wine I'd imbibed the night before.

Mr. Parker hadn't resorted to Byron, but he was sitting far too close for propriety on the settee. Though handsome with dark hair and eyes, he was one whose company I never sought. He had never been summoned for a rescue, but I'd summoned more than one man to rid myself of him.

"I had hoped to secure a dance last night. I was sorry to have missed the opportunity," he murmured. Nothing was overtly inappropriate about the comment, but his tone was too intimate.

Intimate in the same way my mystery gentleman had been, but the effect was revulsion instead of desire.

"I hope you would not think me untoward if I requested the honor of the first two dances at the next ball," he added.

"*Je suis très désolé.* I would not wish to promise something which is not yet mine to give, monsieur. Mama was so unwell last night that we had to say *au revoir* early. Until I am assured of her recovery, I could not possibly offer such a commitment."

Mr. Parker leaned an inch closer and reached for my hand. I shifted forward, moving for my teacup with said hand, gaze firmly fixed on it for deniability.

Jane, darning in the corner by the bell pull, saw it for the signal it was. Out of the corner of my gaze, I caught her two quick pulls of the bell followed by two slow.

I sat back, teacup firmly if not fashionably grasped in both hands.

"If I might be so bold—"

A knock interrupted his certainly too-bold request. Jenkins, the butler, stepped in as I had bade him.

"Pardon me, mademoiselle. Your mother has taken a turn.

I believe she would be much improved if you would sit with her."

The entirety of our household was in want of a raise.

"*Oh non!* I must see to her, right this moment. Would you be so kind as to see Monsieur Parker out? *Merci beaucoup* for the flowers, monsieur."

"Of course, mademoiselle. Mr. Parker, forgive me. Did you arrive by carriage? Should I have it called for you?"

I didn't wait for his response, sweeping out of the room with an appropriate amount of concerned dignity, Jane on my heels. I slipped up the back stairs to avoid any waiting gentlemen who may have arrived. Jenkins would send them on their way with my regrets.

"Well done," I said as soon as Jane and I were closed in my rooms.

"Of course. I am sorry to send the rest of them home early though."

"Nothing for it. I cannot very well send one away and continue to meet with the rest. If they are sent home due to the overly familiar actions of one of their brethren enough times, perhaps a few of the acceptable ones will step up and teach the rest how to behave."

She bit back a chuckle.

The next knock came not ten minutes after I had escaped Mr. Parker's clutches. Jenkins poked his head in.

"All dismissed," he said.

"Thank you. Your rescue was most appreciated."

"Think nothing of it. Is it safe to assume you're no longer home to receive that one?"

"If I'm not home to receive him, I'm not home to receive any of the others... Let us see how he proceeds. Speaking of the others, were there many you had to turn away?"

"Five."

"Did they leave cards?" I was fishing—fishing for a name that certainly wasn't in a stack of callers. Just like there hadn't been a name on the arrangement currently bathed in the morning glow beside my bed, just through the open adjoining door.

"Yes, I've got them somewhere," he replied distractedly, patting his pockets. He found them tucked in his coat and handed them over. The usual suspects—Lucas, James, and the rest. Ellsworth had managed to slip in before Parker in his desperation, but I knew the gentlemen attached to every one of these cards.

"Thank you, Jenkins. I assume Mama is perfectly well?"

"She is. She said to remind you that you're both to dine with Her Grace tonight."

I bit back a sigh. Two sequential evenings at Hasket House... Her Grace would be in need of praise for an evening well hosted. A great deal of praise.

The Duchess of Rosehill was a kind, if dramatic, woman whose feelings required a great deal of management. She was obsessed with all things French, and on occasion, I felt more artifact than guest in her home.

"Do you suppose they've left yet?" I asked.

"I can help them along, if you'd like. Shall I have the carriage readied?"

"Yes, please. I'd like to visit with Mme Bosarge this afternoon."

Jane set to pulling out my favorite walking dress while Jenkins went to remove any stray gentlemen lingering outside.

It was rapidly approaching an hour too late for callers, but Lady Marie Bosarge was too close a family friend to stand on ceremony. A widow of some forty years, she had taken pity on Mama and me for the best part of three years. The difficult years. The long ones between when the funds Mama and I managed to smuggle out of France had long run out and the windfall that came with Grandmere's passing.

I was eight when Mama and I ran. Papa and my brother, Pierre, were to follow a few days later. We took only what we could carry, jewels and coins sewn into our gowns when we boarded the ship. Papa and Pierre never made it to England. In the end, it took months to confirm what we already knew: the mob had taken them.

At first, it was easy to find friends willing to host us. A widow with a young daughter was a sympathetic host. And Mama taught me well. She would trot me out, the tiny French girl with the golden curls and the large green eyes. I would sing and dance with grace and speak in a delicate accent, performing for others' amusement. Charm was our currency, long after the coins ran out.

But even charm wore thin eventually, and we overstayed our welcome more than once. Sometimes that welcome lasted months, and sometimes—such as with Her Grace—it was only a week or two. And then we met Marie. She housed us through three long winters. Right until the day we were able to let the white house with the wrought iron fence and the wisteria trees on King Street.

And I had no doubt that, if Grandmere had not passed, Marie never would have tired of us.

MARIE WAS NOT OVERLY FOND of society, but she was fond of gossip—as was her lady's maid. The girl had a sister with a penchant for eavesdropping who acted as nurse in several great houses.

It was no surprise at all when Marie burst into the entry before the butler had even taken my pelisse.

"Gabriel Hasket? Are you out of your mind?" she demanded.

Gabriel... I tested the name, matching it to the face, the form. It fit.

"Who?" I asked, feigning ignorance for my own amusement. I adored her tendency toward theatrics.

"Gabriel Hasket, Marquis of Rycliffe, eldest son of the Duke of Rosehill! You had some sort of liaison with him. And right on the dance floor I'm told!"

I adored the way she said *marquis*, properly, with none of the *wis* the English added on the end. And Rosehill... That explained his attendance at her ball. And I vaguely recalled the existence of an elder son. But we'd been acquainted with the family for years. How could we have missed an introduction?

Marie widened her eyes significantly, her gaze flicking back to the end of the hall where one eye, brushed by few golden ringlets, peered out behind a corner. Another lady would have given such a gossipy maid her notice, but Marie knew the benefit of controlling the narrative.

"We danced. That is all. It was hardly a liaison. Perhaps we should move this conversation out of the foyer?"

Marie agreed, and out of the corner of my eye I caught a flash as the maid scampered away.

We settled on the sage settee across from the bay window, a tea tray already laid out before us.

"That is not what Lilbet heard," she replied. "She said he held you much too close and you were driven to distraction for the rest of the evening."

That was worrisome. I could not afford to show preference for a single gentleman, even one so interesting as Rycliffe. Besotted women were not mysterious. They were pathetic.

"I was astonished at his crude manner. Nothing more." I enunciated, louder than was my want. A necessary evil to ensure Lilbet could hear from the hall. Certainly she was hovering, gathering intelligence for her sister.

"Crude manners are to be expected from such an unrepentant rake. He is never in polite society. They say he prefers coarser company, but he will not hesitate to seduce a lady if she proves vulnerable."

As I expected, a gentleman in title only. It would be ridiculous to feel disappointment. We'd had but one dance. I had no serious designs on him. He was just... intriguing.

"Well, if he is never in polite society, I doubt we shall meet again. Surely he was only in attendance because his mother was the hostess." Even as I said them, the words felt false. The lie tasted tinny and felt strange in my mouth.

We would meet again. Where or when was a mystery. But it would happen.

"You had best avoid him if you see him again. He singled you out and that cannot be a good thing. He is a known seducer, far too dangerous to flirt with."

I could well believe it. He was dangerous to my composure after a mere dance. The problem with Marie's directive was that I simply had no wish to avoid him. Her intelligence only confirmed what I already suspected... Rycliffe was interesting *because* he was exactly the sort of man I should have nothing to do with.

Lilibet slipped inside, a fresh pot of tea on her tray. The first pot was barely touched and still too hot to sip. She lingered after setting it on the table before us, fussing as she awaited my response.

"Of course. Why should I wish to entertain such a brute?" I said.

The maid still hovered, rearranging the tea things.

Marie, tired of the display and seemingly satisfied with the intelligence Lilibet would report, sighed. "Thank you, Lilibet.

That will be all. And I believe the silver needs to be polished this afternoon. Would you be a dear and see to that?"

The girl's eyes shot to her employer in askance. She was certainly disappointed in the task that would trap her in the kitchens for hours and was far outside of her usual responsibilities. She didn't protest, though, instead pursing her lips as she rose. With feigned distraction, she pulled the door nearly shut. She managed to leave a sliver open.

"Lilibet, the door if you please," Marie called. Finally, the door clicked in the latch.

With an irritated eye roll, she switched to French. "That should satisfy the masses. Now, tell me everything."

A laugh bubbled from my chest, and my cheeks heated.

"He was so unbearably handsome," I replied, in a slightly more stilted French. She tutted at my accent, as she always did, but did not comment.

"The best rakes always are."

"So tall, and broad, and his eyes... He was unbelievably rude, though. And he accused me of holding court with the gentlemen—"

"Which you do," she retorted.

"Of course. But they're not supposed to know that. He told me it would not work on him."

"Did it?" she asked, leaning forward.

"What makes you think I tried?"

"Years of experience." She grinned.

I shot her a significant look. "I did, and it did not. Marie, that has never happened before."

She laughed gayly, her head tipping back with the force of it. "Oh my, I never thought I would live to see the day. You've finally found someone you cannot bat your eyelashes at and get your way."

"It is not amusing," I replied petulantly.

"It is," she insisted. "You're so used to everyone falling in line. You don't know what to do with him."

"I was merely caught off guard. Now that I know what to expect, I will certainly be able to manage him should we meet again."

"I look forward to hearing all of it. What I said before, though, was not entirely for the eavesdropper's benefit. He is a known seducer. Even ladies. You must watch yourself."

"As I said, he shan't get the better of me," I insisted.

"Of course," she replied. Her smirk belied her disbelief.

"He won't."

"I know. I just agreed," she said, her face entirely unconvinced.

With an irritated huff, I resolved to set it aside lest we dance around this topic all afternoon.

She continued, "Now, tell me about the rest of the ball. What ridiculous ensemble did Her Grace don?"

"She is a dear friend of the family. I should not speak ill of her."

"But you will."

"She is still in the throes of her lace obsession. All imported, of course. She is single-handedly funding Napoleon's Empire. But somehow she manages to make it attractive, even in its excess."

"You are too generous, I'm sure. Still all black?"

"And the white. She dresses the children in such as well. It really is quite severe, particularly with their eyebrows."

"Does your Marquis have the brow?" She waggled her own delicate brows in a pitiful demonstration of the over-grown, nearly black brows of Rosehill and his youngest children.

"He has a prominent brow bone, but not the overdrawn eyebrows themselves."

"That is fortunate."

"I'm certain the children will grow into it…"

"You always have been overly optimistic."

"It is the naivety of youth. I'm certain to outgrow it."

That pulled another laugh from her.

"I, for one, hope that you do not. It is refreshing. Tell me, how did you all behave? Which of the gentlemen became your shadow?"

Three

BOLSTERED by an afternoon of excellent tea and even more exceptional conversation, I felt myself equal to another evening at Hasket House.

It wasn't unusual for Her Grace to request our presence—Mama's specifically—the evening after hosting a ball. She required praise for her efforts for several weeks after each event.

What I did not feel equal to was the possibility of *his* company. Gabriel Hasket, Marquis of Rycliffe... It was unlikely he would be present. Almost a certainty—he never had before.

But I couldn't stop myself from dressing with more care than usual. I fussed with the mauve silk ribbons in my hair for too long before dipping my fingers in the rosewater I favored and placing it strategically at my neck and wrists.

When the footman handed Mama and me from the carriage, my stomach was in knots. Still, nothing alighted my spine, nothing to indicate Gabriel was there, that he was watching.

Davina slipped through the door before we reached it,

racing out to greet me. Her Grace's youngest child and only daughter, she had no patience for propriety. The girl flung her arms around my waist, and I stumbled back a step before righting us.

"Cee! The wretched governess wouldn't even let me peer from the stairs last night."

Mama, catching my gaze over the clinging Hasket daughter, nodded that she would precede us in.

"Surely she was merely doing as she was bid," I replied, hoping to spare the poor woman the girl's fury.

"Well, I snuck from the balcony up to the roof and over to the elm there. I watched everyone come and go for hours."

A glance at the offending tree reminded me of its sheer height, thirty feet at least. My hand found my brow in exasperation without conscious thought.

"Let us go inside. I believe there is some time before supper. Surely no one would miss us if we went to your chambers? We can discuss it."

She agreed and pulled me by my wrist. The house was precisely as I left it last evening. White marbled floors and columns offset by black, painted-wood molding and stone steps. Her Grace limited colors to the occasional bold accent.

Davina dragged me past the drawing room, calling into the open door, "Cee and I are going to my rooms," without waiting for a response. I heard Xander, her elder brother's, irritated huff. Somehow in the years I had known the family, I had missed the existence of an eldest brother.

Up two flights, I stumbled along behind the girl and into the former nursery. It seemed her room had been updated to reflect an older, more mature charge. Unlike her mother, Davina was fond of bright colors, which her rooms reflected. Bold blues and greens decorated the chambers with occasional remnants of her childhood scattered about—a loved doll on the settee, a pyramid of blocks on the windowsill.

I could not recall if Davina was two and ten or three, but it was irrelevant. Since she was a child, she very much acted the part of a well-situated widow of some forty or fifty years, albeit a widow with a fondness for toys. She had little care for her studies or reputation and no interest at all in following any of the rules set before her.

The governess would have done better to insist she attend the ball last evening. Davina would have refused and remained in her rooms. That led me to the current concern. Did I report her activities to Her Grace? Surely the governess who lost track of her charge so thoroughly should be terminated, but... it was Davina... and this was certainly not the last governess she would ever have. Whether I reported it or not, the woman would surely give notice or be terminated within the month. They never lasted long with Dav.

Attempting to gather the entire story, I perched on the settee and gathered the doll on my lap. "Tell me again how you escaped your chambers," I said with a sigh.

"I can show you!"

"No!" I bit out, breath catching in my throat. "No, thank you. An explanation is sufficient."

"I went out to the balcony," she said, gesturing behind her to the door. "Then I stepped onto the railing and reached up to the eaves."

My heart caught in my chest—the image of the girl falling to her death far too easy to conjure.

"Then I climbed up to the main part of the roof and walked to the east edge. The tree abuts the roof, and I climbed into the branches. From there I can go up higher and be hidden. You looked so pretty last night, Cee! Like a princess in one of my fairy stories."

This girl was trying to give every single person she met a fit of apoplexy. I was far too young for such a condition.

"Thank you, Davina. That's very nice of you to say. But you know it was very wrong to sneak out, do you not?"

"But Mrs. Meyer wouldn't let me peer from the landing. I wasn't going to go downstairs. I just wanted to see."

I didn't believe that assurance for a single moment.

"No more climbing up that tree, Dav. Promise me."

"Fine. I promise. But I still say Mrs. Meyer was mean."

"She can be mean all she likes, but you still have to mind her. If you're not happy with her treatment of you, you can discuss it with your mother when it's an appropriate time."

"It's never an appropriate time. You know how she is." I knew precisely what Davina meant. Her Grace was a well-meaning woman, but she wasn't particularly well suited to motherhood.

"Then your father."

"Ugh. He's too busy being angry with my brother to care about what I get up to."

"What has Xander done to incur your father's ire?"

"Not Xander—Gabriel. And what hasn't he done? If you ask Father, I'm certain he'd list all the things."

The name was nearly as effective as his presence in disconcerting me. A fluttering began in my chest, swirling warmly.

"I believe I finally had the pleasure of meeting your eldest brother last night."

"Oh, I know. Mother warned him off you after everyone left. And then today, Father summoned him for another scolding. He kept telling Father that you don't possess any accomplishments significant enough to hold his interest. Whatever that means."

My indignation was instantaneous. Of all the... *He* was the one with nothing to hold *my* interest. And *he* was the one who kept staring at *me*.

"You'd have to ask him," I grumbled between clenched

teeth. No matter how offended I was, I wasn't willing to explain his meaning to Davina.

Fortunately, before she pressed me any further, there was a knock on the door. Xander poked his head in.

"You abandoned me to mother's raptures," he accused Davina. Turning to me, he continued. "She's quite pleased with the event, but I believe your mother is running out of things to compliment. She's down to the individual flowers in the arrangements, and she's reached the soapwort."

Oh poor Mama, she was allergic to soapwort. Perhaps her megrim last night hadn't been feigned for my benefit.

"Xander, what did Gabriel mean when he told father that Cee doesn't possess any accomplishments to hold his attention?"

The boy choked on nothing, coughs racking his frame. Though he was not really a boy, not any longer. He was a man of seven and ten, though admittedly a gangly one. And he had received the worst of their father's eyebrows. Dark, rod-straight, and bushy, they overwhelmed his pale skin. Davina's were dark and bold but possessed a more feminine arch. Poor lad.

"As I told you, Davina, none of us can guess what your brother meant by such a thing. You'll have to confront him directly," I said, offering Xander a reprieve he took with grateful, wide eyes.

Unfortunately, Davina was not so easily deterred. "I think you both know what he meant and you're just not telling me."

I sighed, abandoning the pretense. "It was a crass insult about my figure as well as a comment about my general marriageability. And it would amuse me a great deal if you asked him anyway. He deserves to have to explain such an insult to his sister."

"Oh, well why didn't you say so? If it's going to embarrass him, I'll ask."

My heart tripped in my chest. With feigned nonchalance, I asked, "Is he joining us tonight?"

"No, he never dines when father is joining us," she said.

That explained a great deal. Her Grace was not allowed to host without His Grace present. Not after she invited Mama and me to stay with them indefinitely without discussing it with him first. Our stay at Hasket House was brief indeed.

"He'll be at the gaming tables or a match," Xander added. His warm brown eyes were a bit more knowing than I would have liked, or expected from him, really.

I nodded, studiously disinterested. Now that I knew the relation, the resemblance was clear, the brow bone, the dark, unruly hair, the eyes like rich mahogany. Gabriel was a Hasket, through and through.

But he was a Hasket who would not dine at Hasket House tonight. And so my efforts with the hair ribbons had been in vain. Not that I wanted to see him, or dine with him.

I didn't. Not at all.

Four

GRAYSON HOUSE, LONDON - FEBRUARY 13, 1807

DAYS TURNED to weeks turned to months. That prickle of awareness that ran down my spine remained absent. Balls, musicals, dinners—nothing.

The first few events were unbearably tedious. My allure was as palpable as ever, but I found myself summoning a new gentleman with ever-increasing rapidity.

One would think such treatment would offend the *ton*. It seemingly had the opposite effect. The quicker I dismissed them, the more they flocked. Young or old, handsome or plain, titled or third sons, wealthy or poor; it made no difference. One conversation with Gabriel Hasket had ruined me.

Tonight's soiree was courtesy of Lady Agatha Grayson, a middle-aged widow. Her events were always tedious, and she had truly appalling taste in fashions, decor, and perfume. But the food at her events was always exceptional.

I'd been using her signature scent of decaying lilac to avoid her this evening to great success. Like Her Grace, the Duchess of Rosehill, Lady Grayson had an appreciation for the French style. Unlike Her Grace, she hadn't the funds or taste to be so ostentatious in her choices. But she would certainly wish to discuss the improvements—if one could call them that—to her ballroom.

Fortunately, her eldest son was still in the schoolroom. Were there even the slightest chance of a match, she would have thrown him in my path with great determination.

I snuck another cheese-filled pastry and two of the apple tarts when Lady Grayson cornered Mama between sets. Mama, whose sharp look I absolutely did not see, would certainly have words for me when the carriage pulled away tonight. Truly, though, familial love could carry one only so far, and it did not extend to odious conversations with an even more odious woman.

At my side, a rustling sounded in the curtains lining the wall. Rather than a servant slipping between them with more cheese pastries, it was Mr. Montrose. He stalked past me toward the exit. I had a strong suspicion he wouldn't be claiming the supper set he had requested.

All night long, gentlemen had appeared and disappeared, one or two delighted, the others quite despondent.

The rustling curtains split to reveal Mr. Parker, a smug grin on his face. I slipped behind a pillar to avoid his notice.

I would need a replacement for Mr. Montrose, and quickly.

I surveyed my options, eyes settling on a gentleman whose acquaintance I'd not made. He was young, far too young to consider seriously, but youthful was better than repugnant by far.

The gentleman had dark hair and even darker eyes, his lips pulled taut in an uninterested line. He leaned against the wall, one leg crossed over the other.

It took more effort than usual to catch his gaze, as he was far too occupied glaring at everyone in the room to notice me. Once I succeeded, my eyes flitted down, shy and demure. Then I glanced off to the side before flicking my gaze back to his. His lips pulled into a half grin. It was attractive, but not quite as attractive as the half smirk of a certain Hasket brother.

Even though I had his interest, he made no move toward me. I was forced to resort to reaching for my fan, flicking it delicately across the swell of my breasts.

Finally, he straightened slowly, leisurely, before starting toward me. It was impossible to know whether I should be irritated at his nonchalant disinterest or grateful he was less desperate than some of the others.

Stopping just before me, his eyes flicked down to my fan before finding my gaze. "You summoned?" He murmured in a graveled tenor.

"I'm certain I have no idea what you mean, monsieur."

"Of course not. Mademoiselle...?" He was not one to stand on ceremony and wait for an introduction then. That wasn't particularly surprising given his surly, disinterested demeanor.

"Mademoiselle Celine Cadieux. And you?"

"Michael Wayland."

"Of?"

He gestured wordlessly to the surrounding ballroom.

"Wayland?" I questioned. I was quite certain I was in Grayson House. And I knew of no Waylands.

"Bastard," he said simply, without inflection.

He was blunt and entirely unconcerned for propriety, but he was the most intriguing man I'd interacted with in months.

"Well, Mr. Wayland, my partner found himself unwell for the next set." I leaned a little closer, offering him a teasing view.

He raised his brow, eyes flitting down then back to mine. "Who was your partner?"

While I hadn't the slightest idea why he would care, nor why he wasn't delighted at the chance to accompany me to the floor, I had no reason to lie or refuse. "Mr. Montrose."

"Ah… That would be my fault. So sorry for the inconvenience."

"Your fault?"

"He found his wallet a bit lighter this evening."

"So there is a gaming hell."

"Not so much a hell. A study though."

I snapped my fan shut before tapping him on the shoulder. He was rather slow to fulfill his role, but he would suffice for a set.

"Alas, I still find myself without a partner," I explained, hoping understanding would dawn.

"Best bat your lashes elsewhere. I don't dance."

"Not even for me?" I asked with a flirtatious smile.

"Not even for you. And I won't be attending supper. You'll have to find a different escort."

That was a disappointment. He was the least objectionable option, and more than tolerable, if a little slow to heel. But I could appreciate his honesty, rather than wasting my time.

"Well, I should not wish to dance with a newly made pauper. Who have you left with a fortune intact?"

Before he could respond, I felt it. The searing tingles dancing down my spine. And I knew without a doubt, without a word, who was at my back.

"Me," the familiar, sensuous, silky voice said. The word caressed my neck and shoulders, warming me from inside out like the finest liquor. A warm bergamot scent enveloped me.

"Rycliffe," Mr. Wayland acknowledged the form behind me.

"Wayland. Don't you have a viscountess to avoid?"

I refused to turn. I could not allow him to affect me as he had before. I would not.

"Low…" Wayland grumbled in response.

"Leave us." The sumptuous, honeyed voice behind me brokered no argument.

Wayland, unintimidated, rolled his eyes before nodding to me in acknowledgment.

"It was a pleasure to make your acquaintance, Mademoiselle."

He turned and made his way back to his wall where a tall, gangly footman waited for him.

"At least your taste has improved somewhat," the man—Gabriel—said.

Left with no other choice, I took a fortifying breath before turning to face him. Once again, he was pressed too close to my back, and now my chest. I stepped back to find the ever-present smirk calling his lips home.

"I'm somewhat impressed you were able to lure that one," he added. "He has as little interest in polite society as it has in him."

Gabriel—Rycliffe—was even more unbearably handsome than I recalled. More disheveled too. His cravat had been loosened and retightened lazily. It was so haphazard that I could see the dip of his Adam's apple when he swallowed. I was possessed by the utterly inane desire to lick it—*Focus.*

"My dance card has an unexpected space on it," I said. The words escaped without permission.

"Who?"

"Montrose."

He chuckled. "Yes, he would be feeling poorly."

"How much?"

"Seven-thousand pounds."

"Excuse me?" I half asked, half spat.

"Well, we don't play for shillings."

"And you always play for such sums?"

"Usually. Sometimes we play for favors, information, and

other assets. Whatever we have on hand," he explained with a disinterested shrug.

Without asking permission he wrapped his overly large hand around my shoulder and once again manhandled me to the dance floor with nothing resembling a request.

"What are you doing?" I asked, indignation spilling out inelegantly.

"I should think that would be obvious. I'm dancing with you." He moved my hand to his shoulder before slipping his own scandalously low on my waist.

The gossamer lavender fabric of my gown was flimsy, nonexistent really. Something about the pitiful barrier made his strength, his heat all the more apparent.

I shook away the thought. "Are you incapable of asking me to dance like a proper gentleman?"

"Yes," he said. "And you don't want a proper gentleman."

"You and your presumptions. Of course I want a proper gentleman. One who can behave with decorum and gentility." My voice had gone a touch shrill again. I needed to get ahold of myself. My pulse pounded, and my breath was too heavy— mocking the confidence I needed to put him in his place.

"No, you don't. You want *me*," he replied, smirk deepening. His lips were unfairly pink and lush. Such a boorish man should not have such pretty lips.

"I want nothing less than you. You've accosted me twice."

His eyes trailed down to my lips before flicking back to mine. "If you don't want me, then why have you not summoned a rescue? As you said, twice we've danced and spoken, and twice you've been unable to take your eyes off me."

"I cannot trust you long enough to take my eyes off you." At least that part was true, even if sharper and more pathetic in tone than I would have wished.

"Oh, of course. What if I promise to behave long enough

for you to beckon a proper gentleman—one brave enough to face me?"

I gaped, floundering without a response.

"You should do it. I won't make the offer again," he added.

"I would not wish to draw greater attention to your scandalous behavior."

He chuckled, the grin pulling to one corner of his mouth in that newly familiar way that left my stomach flipping—in frustration, of course.

"Such a lovely little liar. You don't want to leave my arms. But that's quite all right. I don't want to let you go." He pulled me impossibly closer, pulling my waist into his. He maintained a mere inch between us, and through layers of silk and petticoat and waistcoat, he still seared my skin.

His eyes were mahogany tonight, his pupils large in the dim lighting. He dragged them along my form as though the fabric of my gown wasn't there at all. The swell of my breasts, the nip of my waist, the forbidden place between my legs—his gaze was tangible. I shouldn't allow it.

I'd had plans, intentions, for the next time we met. They were long gone, flown from my head. None of my tricks or protestations had made the slightest impact on him. Months of preparation—determination to be unaffected—all for nothing.

Because he wasn't wrong.

Swirling alongside what I knew to be lust, even if I was reluctant to term it such, was a sense of safety, security. There was danger in him, certainly. I wasn't oblivious to the way the masses eyed him. But there was protection too. I did not have to perform for him—it wouldn't work anyway.

He tugged me even closer, my cheek brushing against the fabric of his waistcoat.

"If I were a better man, I would let you go. I thought I could manage just the once... I thought it would be enough..."

he murmured, the words barely audible. I suspected they were more for his benefit than mine.

"Why is that?"

"Surely you know by now. Someone would have told you, warned you."

"You are a notorious rake. I've been informed of that."

"Then you know why I shouldn't be claiming you. Publicly. Blatantly."

His hand dipped lower on my waist, burning me. It was precisely the sort of thing he should not be doing.

"An unrepentant seducer would not be concerned for my reputation," I said slowly, my cheek still pressed half an inch from his chest.

The hand on my waist slid up, directing me back from his chest to meet his gaze again.

"I don't seduce innocents. Not any longer." His tone was fierce, and so was his gaze. Ochre eyes bored into mine, willing me to believe that much at least.

The insistence led to an obvious question, one I was nearly certain I already knew the answer to.

"But you have?"

"Yes." His eyes shuttered, the fire doused.

"Why no longer?"

"The consequences are too great."

"For whom?" I asked.

"For her."

He was speaking from experience, and that experience was filled with regret. There was no other explanation for that tone. And I knew without a doubt there was some lady out there entirely lost to polite society. And he was responsible.

I clung desperately, hoping for reassurance when the next question escaped me. "And you concern yourself with that?"

"I do. And if you're smart, you will stay away."

I was smart. Usually. But a second meeting hadn't made

him any less appealing. In fact, I was almost certain it had done the opposite.

He'd ruined other gentleman for me. He was right. I didn't want them. I had no wish to dance with a gentleman with proper manners and dull attentions.

"You approached me. Both times." I reminded him. "And you watched me before that."

His brow caught in surprise. "You know about that?"

Of course. I've been aware of you far longer than I knew of you.

"I do," I said without further explanation.

"I should stay away. I know that. You're a lady—entirely off limits. But I don't seem to be capable of it. I'm not in the practice of self-denial, so it will have to come down to you."

Heart pounding in my chest, I laid out the fundamental flaw in his plan. "For that to work, you would have to stop seeking me out."

The last strains of the waltz settled in the air between us, still a mere, heated inch.

He was going to vanish again. I was more certain of that than I was that the sun would rise tomorrow.

"Our dance is ending again. It has been a pleasure. I'm afraid I won't be able to escort you to dinner. I am more than certain you can find another suitor without much effort." With those words he released me and backed away with the same caution one would give a wild beast.

I was once again struck by the audacity of this man.

"You cannot be serious?"

"I am. I'm afraid this is goodbye, Celine."

He turned, slipping back into the crowd again. He was gone before I could chastise him for the use of my Christian name. Before I could beg him to say. Set him down for his behavior. Kiss him.

Five

EVERY BITE of mutton took longer than the last to swallow. And even more effort to do so without an unladylike display. Mama was right; we absolutely should have declined this invitation.

Lady Bracewit, our hostess, was only seven and ten. She'd wed her husband a mere month ago, a lecherous baron nearly thrice her age. On more than one occasion, I'd been forced to dodge his advances before he trapped the young miss. Ordinarily, that would be more than sufficient to ensure I never set a toe in his household. But I just hadn't the heart to see her first event as hostess be as great a disappointment as her marriage was sure to be.

Even so, I was beginning to see that the event would have met with greater success had no one attended. Then no one would be able to blame their distressed digestive systems on the newlywed.

I bit down on another carrot in hopes of a reprieve from the mutton. Unseasoned and nearly raw but still more palatable than the meat.

The table was nearly silent, save for the clank and scrape of knives and forks on plates. Everyone was trying to choke down the meal as quickly as possible.

The baron must have had some say in the seating arrangements because I was at his side near the head of the table with Mama beside me. It was an unusual arrangement and one that made an already repulsive meal even more unpleasant.

Fortunately, I was seated across from an earl whose acquaintance I'd never had the pleasure of making. Unlike our host, he was young, handsome, and unbelievably tall. Truly, it was a wonder he didn't injure himself on doorways.

His tousled blond locks framed his clear blue eyes, and the dimple on his chin lent interest—even more than his height allotted.

At least I had something pleasant to look upon while I poisoned myself at society's directive.

The baron leaned over his plate, his eyes firmly fixed on the cut of my gown.

"Isn't my wife a fine young thoroughbred, Miss Cadieux?" He asked with a quick leer at his wife before returning his beady gaze to my bosom.

Truth be told, she was rather silly, and she bore a striking resemblance to the butler at her father's home. But she was sweet, and I wouldn't allow him to disparage her.

"She's a fine young lady, my lord. Any man would be lucky to have such a wife." I neglected to correct him on my title. Whether it survived the revolution was a subject for debate anyway.

"Oh yes, a lady, but what is a lady but a human of fine breeding? Much like a thoroughbred."

Why is it always horses?

"Well, I hope you see more benefit in your wife than speed on a racetrack and the ability to breed. She's quite an accomplished pianist, if I remember correctly. And her watercolors are lovely." I had no idea if those were accomplishments owed to Lady Bracewit, but it seemed safe to assume her husband didn't either.

"Mere varnish. All that's needed of a lady is a good pedigree and birthing hips. If she comes in a pretty package, all the better. Don't you agree, Lord Champaign?" He directed the last of that repugnant speech to the unfamiliar gentleman across from me.

"Not at all. The varnish, as you call it, is precisely what makes us different from beasts," Lord Champaign replied. His jaw shifted, lips pursed in irritation that had nothing to do with the inferior meal.

"Ah, I forgot. You're still young, my boy. You found yourself a dairy maid or some such thing during the harvest then? They're useful, for a time. But your wife needs to have good breeding. Otherwise your children will be degenerates. Surely your father taught you this before he passed. I'd be happy to provide guidance if he wasn't able to impart that wisdom."

"My father provided more than sufficient guidance. I'm in no need of additional wisdom," he said, spearing a piece of mutton and shoving it in his mouth, putting an end to the conversation.

I watched the regret shift over his face as he chewed, and chewed, and chewed. My teeth caught my lower lip, holding my smile at bay. It would not do to laugh at a seemingly intelligent, objectively handsome earl.

My gaze dipped to my plate before I flicked my eyes up beneath lowered lashes. And there I met blue. Lord Champaign's lip curled back in a crooked smile.

The following course was occupied in dodging Lord Bracewit's breeding plans for both wife and horse, consuming as little of the meal as possible, and in silent flirtation with Lord Champaign. His quiet interest was marked yet respectful.

He offered a raised brow when Lord Bracewit detailed his

current scheme to purchase studding rights in conjunction with some lord or mister I couldn't recall, to breed the greatest racing horse of all time.

"Forgive me, Lord Bracewit, but it seems you intend to purchase stud rights to a particularly fine racehorse and breed it to your own particularly fine mare. Is that correct?" I asked.

"Indeed, it is. In fact—"

"Is that not what every other gentleman involved in the breeding of racehorses is doing at precisely this moment?"

"Ah, but not with this stud," he replied, failing to note the derision in my tone.

Lord Champaign cut in. "But if it is the best, surely they are. Or is it somehow a hidden gem?"

"A hidden gem to be sure."

I seized on the opportunity. "In that case, perhaps we should change the subject. We wouldn't want anyone to over-hear about this secret stud and hound the owner for the horse's... prowess."

Lord Champaign choked on his sip of wine, coughing roughly.

"Would you believe, I hadn't considered that," Lord Bracewit said.

"Absolutely, I would."

The earl caught his lower lip between his teeth, fighting back a laugh. Lord Bracewit, not nearly witty enough to catch my meaning, moved on to shooting. If it wasn't horses it was shooting, usually on horseback.

Just before the final course, if something so inedible could be called a course, a footman dipped to whisper into Lord Bracewit's ear.

"Send him to my study. I'll be there in a moment," he replied, dismissing the footman. He shoved the chair from the table with a discordant scratching. To the entire table, he said, "Pardon me, ladies, gentlemen. I need to step away on an urgent matter of business. Please don't wait for me to enjoy your meal."

As if enjoyment was a possibility.

He strode from the room, filled with purpose.

"What do you suppose that was about?" Lord Champaign asked.

"Probably has the stud in his study. That's why they call it a study, is it not?"

He laughed, easy and free. "Do you know, I think I remember something to that effect."

"The question is whether the mare is in there too, or if he plans to do that part—"

"Celine," Mama cut me off sharply under her breath. Apparently she hadn't entirely forgone chaperone duties after her third glass of wine.

"—later," I finished.

A glance at Mama told me she knew precisely how I'd meant to finish that sentence and that my recovery wasn't sufficient to save me from a lecture in the near future.

"Tell me, Lord Champaign. Where are you from?" That was a safe question. One Mama surely couldn't find fault with.

The answer, as it turned out, was a rather dull eight miles south of the city. With a bit of encouragement, the earl fell just like the rest of the *ton*. He was reduced to telling me of his estate and the surrounding lands. While I hadn't spent much time out of London, even I could not be interested in the landscape so near my home.

"—and I've just begun work on an observatory. The telescope—"

The newly built observatory might have been slightly more interesting than the land, if only I hadn't felt *it* again, that peculiar sensation of being watched so specific to one Gabr—Lord Rycliffe.

My chest tightened, nearly painfully.

Not again. I would not, could not, fall to pieces at his mere presence. I shook my head, stabbing at a bite of some sort of pear dessert as a cover. Immediately, I regretted the bite as I worked to chew thoroughly before swallowing the slimy mass.

I forced myself to focus on Lord Champaign, to appear interested in his talk of curved mirrors and how they were polished. At least it wasn't horses.

"How does that work?" I asked at a break in his speech. It seemed to do the trick and he carried on, clearly passionate about his project.

Just as quickly as the sensation arrived, it vanished.

Lord Rycliffe was gone. And with him, the knot in my chest loosened, but everything took on a duller, dim hue and tone. As though I were under water.

The rest of the evening dragged on, unbearably tedious through the distorted, colorless world I now inhabited.

When I fell asleep that night, it was to the memory of sensual touches and dark, burning gazes.

Six

HASKET HOUSE - LONDON - FEBRUARY 27, 1807

IF MAMA NOTICED my reluctance to join her on a visit to Hasket House, she made no mention of it. She also kindly chose to ignore the extra—likely fruitless—efforts I put toward my coiffure.

Upon our arrival, we were thrust into Her Grace's favorite drawing room. The oversize windows faced the street, allowing her the best view, and providing it for all who passed by. Every inch of this room was to Her Grace's taste. The woman somehow managed to combine elements that were elegance personified—delicate settees, sleek curtains, gracefully carved wood furnishings—into an exhibition of true ostentatiousness.

Today, she had fashion plates spread across every available crisp, white furnishing and unblemished dark-stained mahogany table. That would explain the urgency of her summons then. Her Grace thought France the peak of taste, and I could not fault her for such understanding. But how she managed to receive so many shipments from the country was beyond belief. She was single-handedly responsible for a smuggling operation. It was the only explanation.

"Oh, my dear friends! You simply must examine the latest plates. I informed you that white muslin would be de rigueur for some time to come," she exclaimed, thrusting one of the plates at Mama. "And see here, that train I suggested you include in your little design, Celine," she pointed excitedly at a plate, which did, indeed, show a much more significant train than was presently à la mode.

"*Oui*, you are quite right as always," Mama replied with Her Grace's usual due praise.

"Perhaps I will see if the modiste can add it to the lavender gown she is making up," I added. I plucked a nearby plate from the desk near the door, examining it with feigned interest. The etching was stained a ghastly yellow. At least Her Grace would never suggest that shade.

Her younger son, Xander, wandered in, biscuit in hand, wincing at the sheer number of plates.

"Where did you find all of these?" he asked, gesturing with the biscuit.

"I have my ways, darling."

"Perhaps we could consolidate them? Before Father sees?"

"Why would your dear father protest such delightful little extravagances?"

"There are quite a lot of little extravagances, Mother. And I suspect they're accompanied by some larger extravagances already with the modiste. It's just that—you know Father doesn't understand fashion. And Gabe is here. You know how Father will feel about that."

My knees wobbled for a moment before I remembered myself. It was always a possibility, however remote. I steeled my spine and pulled my shoulders back. I would not be turned into a teetering calf by the mere knowledge that the man was in residence. That was something other ladies did—ladies I had no interest in emulating.

"Dear Gabriel will bid us a tearful adieu well before our

great patriarch returns," Her Grace retorted. Her son sighed, stuffing the last of the biscuit into his mouth before snatching a fashion plate of his own to examine.

Under his breath, Xander added, "Of course, because Gabriel never does anything with the express purpose of needling Father."

I'd known Rycliffe wasn't close with the family—several year's acquaintance without coming across him proved that very point. And his presence did needle me. But his own father?

Xander handed me one of the plates, this one depicting a gentleman. "What do you think of the pantaloons instead of the breeches?"

I wasn't well versed in men's fashions. I knew what looked fine on a particular gentleman, though I knew nothing of the latest trends. But I always tried for Xander. If I did not, his mother would insist on the most audacious choices.

"They seem as though they would be more comfortable. But it does diminish the line of the leg somewhat. What about these collars? They're getting quite high, are they not?"

He nodded, thoughtful, while he plucked at the fine wool of his dark breeches with his free hand.

"Xander, darling, come examine this one with me. I particularly admire the lapel," his mother called.

Abandoned for the moment, I found it more difficult to ignore the intelligence I'd gleaned and focus on the veritable cornucopia that had arrived from my homeland.

Before I could give it due consideration, my hands went to the bodice of my gown, tugging it to lay in the most flattering way. And then, in one of the worst ideas I'd ever had, I called out, "I'm going to say hello to Davina," as I slipped through the door.

The hall was more of the same, elegance paired with other elegances in a way that flattered none. With no actual direction, I trailed down the hall, dragging a fingertip along the extravagant wallpaper toward Davina's rooms. In the brief time we'd stayed in the house, I'd become quite familiar with the back stairs. They were the closest to the kitchen and the delightful cheeses Her Grace insisted on.

Now, I took them two at a time, unwilling to lose my nerve. The family wing was no more inviting than the drawing room, but I found the cracked door of Davina's new rooms—without a balcony—at the end of the corridor easily.

What I didn't expect to see was the massive form of Gabriel Hasket, Marquis of Rycliffe hunched over the small table strewn with tea things across from his sister. His back was angled toward me, but I knew those shoulders anywhere.

"Now you call the main," he patiently explained, as he handed her a pair of dice.

"And I can pick any number between five and nine?"

"Yes," he replied.

"Seven," she said, a proud little dance in her seat accompanying the pronouncement. At two or three and ten, Davina was never still, always shifting for a better view, to be heard, to have her questions answered.

"Good. Now you put up the stakes," he added, passing a few shillings along the table to her. Good lord, the man was teaching a child to gamble. I *should* find Her Grace and alert her to the corruption occurring under her roof. I *should* put a stop to it myself.

But Davina wore her delight in the flush of her cheeks and the brightness of her smile. "This seems an awful lot like chance. Where is the skill?"

"Hazard is a lot of chance, it's true. But the real skill is reading the man across from you."

"Ladies aren't allowed into hells," she muttered, her grin slipping.

"Not yet. But you're like me. We find trouble," he whispered conspiratorially. "And besides, once you come of age, you'll need to read men anyway. And they're all going to underestimate you. Every last one."

"They are?" she asked, wonder slipping through.

"Yes. In fact, I insist that you cannot marry a man if he underestimates you. You must find one who knows the incredible things you're capable of and who adores you for it, not in spite of it." I couldn't see his face, but I could hear the earnest sincerity in his tone. And so could Davina, if the adoration in her expression was an indication.

Suddenly, a frown crossed her face. "What if I never find one? You said it yourself, there aren't many."

"Then you'll live with me. You and I will turn the *ton* on its end."

And with that, elation was back in her eyes. "Do you promise?"

"I promise. But first, you'll need to learn hazard."

She nodded with all the solemnity her tiny body could muster. I took a step back, intending to leave them to their game, when she asked, "Gabriel? Does Celine underestimate you? Is that why you said she hasn't any accomplishments to hold your interest?"

Her brother choked on whatever was in the delicate teacup. While he was racked with coughs, her eyes slid to mine, pinning me in place.

"Are you all right?" she asked her brother with false concern.

"Where did you hear that?" he wheezed.

"I heard you say it to Father. And when I told Cee you said it, she said I should ask you."

"You told—*cough*—you told Celine I said that?"

"I did, and she didn't seem pleased. She's very accomplished. In truth, I don't know what other accomplishments you could want from a lady."

And that was the precise moment I knew Davina had always known exactly what her brother had meant by the comment. And I knew that I, too, had underestimated her. It was hidden, nearly invisible, but a smile hovered at the edge of her lips. Delightfully devious, that one.

"I just wanted—no, Lady Celine has all the accomplishments any man could ever want. It's just, you know how Father can be."

I knew I was accomplished in nearly every way worth mentioning. And any *accomplishments* I was missing could easily be gained after a wedding night. But it had something tightening in my chest to hear it.

"Then she underestimates you?"

He took another sip of tea, which I suspected held more than tea. "Perhaps, but I rather like that about her. It has been a long time since anyone did. My reputation precedes me, you know." I felt the heat rise in my cheeks at the thought.

"Do you underestimate her, then?"

"No. I suspect I might be the only one in this damned town who doesn't." Now that he'd said it, I realized it was entirely likely he was right, and I wasn't quite certain what to do with that. I wasn't Davina, who was bold and brash to a fault. I was adaptable. Managing a husband who underestimated me could very well be the easiest thing in the world.

"Then why have you not asked her to marry you?" she questioned, her quizzical brow raised.

"I—it's not that simple. I'm not the marrying kind."

"I think you're afraid to put up the stakes," she challenged, her gaze flicking to mine once more.

I caught the edge of his muttered, "too smart for your own bloody good," before I turned and slipped away down the hall, more confused than ever before.

Seven

THEATRE AT DRURY LANE, LONDON - MARCH
4, 1807

THERE HAD BEEN no recurrence of the needling awareness in the weeks since my eavesdropping. No smooth baritone purr in my ear. And worst of all, no infuriating smirk. For a mannerism I considered so irritating, it was disconcerting to find myself longing for it. There was little surprise in the absence, though; he had all but promised our second dance would be our last.

But I didn't want it to be our last.

Thus far, he had made all the decisions for our interactions, the purview of a gentleman. I enjoyed my own little game within those rules, allowing men to think their actions were their own whilst bending them to my will.

But the truth of it was, if he did not wish to be summoned, I had no power to drag him before me. If he chose to remain on the outskirts of polite society, I could not force him to move in my circles. And that, more than anything, was the irritation. Certainly not the attraction I felt to him. That was nothing more than I felt for any other passably handsome gentleman, not at all more significant.

He'd ruined my favorite game though. Instead of exhilarating, it was exhausting.

And *that* was unforgivable.

I jumped at the chance to attend the theater with Marie and Mama, rather than endure another in an endless round of balls with the same uninteresting faces and bland conversations.

I adored the theater. I often thought that, were my circumstances different, I could have been an exceptional actress. After all, I had been acting my entire life. I really ought to have been paid for my efforts.

Tonight was *The Castle Spectre*. I had seen it before, but I never came to the theater for the performances. No one did. At least not the one on stage. Something about the theater turned everyone into actors. We all sat in our seats and played the part of interested observers whilst actually studying the audience.

Mama was accosted and captured by Lady Grayson immediately upon arrival, but Marie and I abandoned her to her fate and escaped to Marie's box.

We took our places, fitting seamlessly into the role of patrons, observing the stage on occasion, studying the audience with interest, making the occasional teasing comments.

Then I felt it. That sense of anticipation. That creeping awareness slipping up my spine.

He was here.

I refused to dignify his stare with an acknowledgment. He had abandoned me; he deserved no such attentions. I did not straighten. I did not scan my gaze eagerly over the crowd.

Instead I turned my attention to the stage, offering the performance somewhat more attention than it deserved.

The tingling remained, gaining in intensity.

After minutes that could only be described as hours, there was a break. Marie left to retrieve Mama from Lady Grayson's clutches. I remained, feigning some excuse about avoiding the woman's perfume.

As the door shut, I slipped up into a darkened corner of the box, hidden from the view across and below by a curtain. Safely tucked into the shadows where I knew he could no longer stare, my muscles unfurled and I sank back into the scratchy velvet chair.

Using the thick, red velvet for cover, I surveyed the boxes across from mine. Presumably he was there.

One, two, three—all empty. The fourth was overfilled, perhaps the occupants of boxes one through three had made their way there.

Then I caught a glimpse of dark hair and a broad build in the seventh. Gabrie—Lord Rycliffe's head was tipped down as he whispered into the ear of the petite blonde pressed too close next to him.

She was perfectly respectable in dress and appearance. I had gowns with a lower-cut bodice. But I knew. Perhaps it was their easy familiarity with each other. Perhaps the way she adjusted the knot of his cravat possessively. His words from weeks before rang through me. *"No innocents."* She knew him. Personally. Intimately. Carnally.

She knew him in all the ways he had no interest in allowing me to know him.

My stomach gave an uncomfortable lurch at that realization. It was jealousy. I was not so delusional to mistake the feeling for missish prudishness.

His hand was wrapped around her upper arm, encompassing the entirety of it the same way it had mine. I loathed the sight.

His hands did not belong on her. I refused to trail that thought to completion, to consider where they did belong.

Mama and Marie burst into the box in a flurry of French complaints. I moved to join them, hoping to make it look as if

I had been with them. If a certain gentleman with dark eyes, a crooked grin, and his hands all over a trollop had noted my absence, I cared not. If I tugged the bodice of my gown slightly lower to display my less than ample bosom to best advantage, that was a coincidence.

Resolutely, I stared at the stage, offering him only my cheek. The one permanently displayed to him. Because I was absolutely riveted by this performance.

Out of the corner of my eye, I saw him lean forward as if he'd dropped something. He then settled back in his seat slowly.

At first, I thought nothing was amiss. But the way his arm slipped into his companion's lap, the way she moved in her seat...

My inexperienced mind refused to draw the obvious conclusion, and in my confusion, I forgot myself. I turned to face him. At the precise moment comprehension dawned, his gaze caught mine across the theater.

Abruptly, I stood, nearly tripping in my attempt to escape, in my desperation for the reprieve of the hall. I urged Mama and Marie to remain, tossing them some explanation about needing fresh air. It was true. The box was too hot, the air too thin.

My cheeks burned with something like shame, or hurt, or some other feeling I was less eager to explore or name.

I found the wall for support and pressed a hand to my chest to slow my breaths, my heart. This should not be so affecting. He was nothing to me. I had danced with hundreds of men, and they all meant nothing. He was no different. He was not special. He was nothing to me. Nothing.

After several moments of catching my breath, I found myself equal to the prospect of returning to the box. I could only hope my face was not as flushed as it felt. I offered my companions some excuse, delicately implicating my menses, which I knew neither lady would examine too closely.

I found my seat once again, this time with more nonchalance and serenity than should have been possible to exude. I did not risk a glance in his direction.

Minutes passed with nothing, no tangible burn of his eyes on me. It must have been nearly half an hour before I blinked away from the stage, flicking a glance across the theater.

He was gone.

She was gone.

The box was empty.

They had probably gone to a hallway to fornicate. An alleyway. A sewer. Where they belonged.

Neither returned for the rest of the performance. The end of the play brought more relief than I had ever known.

The usual production followed as we returned to the carriage. Greetings of Her Grace, the Duchess of Sutton. Another near run-in with the Viscountess Grayson. Various suitors who required placation.

When we finally stepped out into the London night, the line of carriages was much shorter.

And there he was.

Not out in the open, but the awareness, the gooseflesh running down my spine, was back in full force.

And I was tired. Too tired to feign disinterest. Too tired to act as though I had no idea he was there. Watching me.

At last, I found him, shrouded in darkness at the edge of the theater. Nearly invisible. Thankfully alone.

There was no pretending this time. My emerald eyes found his ochre ones, even in the near total blackness. He took a singular step forward, the left side of his face tipped to the light, the other shrouded in shadow.

Instead of the smirk I expected, there was something

forlorn in his countenance. Or perhaps that was wishful thinking on my part.

He swallowed, his throat working harshly against his loosened cravat. It sounded insane, even to my own rational mind, but in that moment, I could read him. As sure as I could read words on a page.

"It had to be done. I am not a good man. You needed to know, needed to see."

And he was right. He had well and truly shattered any illusions I'd held. Girlish fantasies of the power of my beauty, charm, and grace to redeem the irredeemable rake.

I could only guess at what he read in my expression. *"You could not have picked a more hurtful way to show me." "You disgust me." "What does she give you that I cannot?"*

From behind me, inside the carriage, Mama called out to me. Eyes still locked on his, I took a step back, then another, before turning and stepping into the carriage without looking back.

His exit.

I understood then why he'd done it. There was something sensual, powerful about the simple maneuver.

LATE THAT NIGHT, long after the rest of the house was abed, I remained perched on the window seat in my boudoir. Staring out at the empty unending length of the early morning King Street below.

It was too dark to see, and I would never be able to prove it. But in the pitch of night, invisible from the safe perch of my room, my gaze met a dark, wretched one.

It was many long minutes, perhaps as long as an hour, before the heat of that gaze left me. Only then did I blow out the candle beside me and turn in for the night.

Eight

IT SEEMED LEOPOLD BENNETT, Lord Champaign, was the least objectionable option.

After that night at the theater, I hadn't a single sighting of Lord Rycliffe. And that was quite all right with me. Truly.

But his arrival and subsequent disappearance had served as an awakening. My charms, such as they were, were more fleeting than I had thought. They would not withstand a serious scandal.

Now presented with the task of finding an acceptable gentleman to wed, Lord Champaign seemed to rise above the rest. He was handsome, certainly, though perhaps too tall. On the dance floor, he cut a fine figure. And far from a teasing smirk, his smiles were genuine and his eyes crinkled with delight.

His reputation was spotless as well. Even Marie could find no objections to him. Her maid had a story of the man rescuing a kitten from a tree. While I could well believe him capable of it—if only because he was so tall that it likely required no more effort than the raising of his arm—it seemed far-fetched. Or, it had a month ago.

Now, when he greeted Mama and I warmly, I knew it was no act.

"Am I still to have the pleasure of this set, Lady Celine?" he asked, his gaze flitting between Mama's and mine. He waited for her nod and my own before escorting me onto the floor.

Once there, he placed me a proper distance away and kept his hands in entirely decent places. He was everything I *should* want in a husband. In short, he was everything that Gabriel Hasket, Marquis of Rycliffe, was not.

The set proceeded without incident, and after applauding the musicians, he tucked my hand back in the crook of his arm and led me back to Mama, exactly as was expected.

"I wonder, if it's not too bold, if I might request the supper set as well? If you're not otherwise engaged."

I considered it. Two sets, the first and the supper set, was a statement of intent. Was it a statement I was ready to make?

His eyes were clear and blue and his countenance open. He would accept whichever answer I gave him without complaint. But, as was proper, a no would be the end of the first tentative strains of this courtship.

I opened my mouth, fully intending to agree to the set, to agree to the ramifications of it. But my voice wouldn't cooperate. Nothing came out. Instead, I nodded, swallowing harshly. His beaming smile dulled some of the flutters in my chest.

Lord Champaign released me at Mama's side. "Would either of you care for a drink?"

"That would be delightful. I thank you, Lord Champaign," Mama answered, barely glancing his way. Her eyes were on me. He set off, task in hand.

"Cherie? What is it?" she asked me in hushed French.

"He... he asked for the supper set," I answered in numb French.

"Ah. And you are... unsure?"

"Ye—no. I mean to say, he's a good choice. Any woman would be lucky to have such a husband."

"I agree. If he asked for your hand, I would have no objections. But is this what you want?"

Before I could reply, Lord Champaign returned with three glasses triangled in his hands. Mama undertook the burden of conversation, allowing me a few more moments to breathe.

Far too soon, Mr. Ellsworth arrived to claim his set. Lord Champaign nodded at him politely before the man guided me to the floor. Perfectly proper Lord Champaign.

He always did that. Allowed other gentlemen to claim me for sets with nary a raised brow.

And so it went. I danced with Ellsworth, Mr. Price, Lord Worthington, an unending set with Mr. Parker, and finally I was returned to Lord Champaign. More resigned than ever.

So much so that when I felt the familiar shiver run down my spine, my steps did not falter in the slightest.

But it was no surprise when my next partner grasped my hand and banded his other arm low around my waist. The weight of it was suffocating.

"Champaign? You cannot be serious," the husky words slipped from Gabriel—Lord Rycliffe's—mouth, smooth as cream.

"I hardly think it is any of your concern, my lord."

Elegantly, I passed into a new set of arms, thin, tobacco-scented, and unappealing. Barron James.

After a turn, I made my way back to my partner's arms, where Lord Champaign's smiles remained easy and entirely unconcerned about the grave marquis whose embrace I was soon to return to.

Lord Rycliffe's intensity had not diminished with the separation. "Celine, he will bore you."

"I did not give you leave to use my Christian name, sir," I retorted with as much venom as I could muster without attracting undue attention. "And I'm certain you are correct. At least, if your definition of *interesting* includes public indecency. Mine, however, does not."

I risked a glance up at him for the first time since the dance began. He was peering down at me with hurt worn into his expression. Irritation snapped through me. What right had he to be hurt?

I endured three more partners through gritted teeth, including poor Lord Champaign, who deserved a less-distracted partner.

Then I found myself back in Lord Rycliffe's arms once more. I continued as if there had been no interruption.

"You have made it perfectly clear, sir, that you have no serious designs on me. You can hardly object to my finding a gentleman who does."

"C—" he cut himself off before I could check him. "Mademoiselle Cadieux, he cannot make you happy."

"And having made me nothing but miserable in every one of our interactions, you are the expert in what will make me happy?"

I was handed off, back to the moist Barron James. The exertion of the dance added to his usual perspiration. This was why I preferred the waltz, a singular partner with whom one could remain close and converse.

The set ended before I was returned to Gabriel yet again. If I made a show of sliding my hand along Lord Champaign's arm possessively while he escorted me to the table, no one could prove it.

At supper, my suitor paid me all due attention, even if some of that attention revolved around star charts.

Astonishingly, Gabr—Lord Rycliffe—remained for supper. He was seated across from me and to the left a few seats. His eyes never left my form. Not that I saw him. Because

I wasn't looking. But it was simply impossible to ignore the gaze of a man in lust.

It was two full courses before he broke me. Two courses before my eyes flicked his direction without my permission and met his.

And I was done.

He was everything I shouldn't want. But the way he made me feel... The connection... It was undeniable.

I would be his, one way or another. He would be mine. No matter how I tried to lie to myself, we were inevitable, Gabriel and me. We would collide, and I could only hope we would not destroy everything around us in the resulting explosion.

My all-too-trusting suitor was quick to believe my assurances that I would return to the table momentarily.

The Sutton home featured a lovely patio just inside the gardens. It was too dark to discern many of the blooms, but their fragrance was lovely. I had forgone my wrap in favor of a subtle escape. If my prediction was correct, I would not be chilled for long.

The moon was full and close enough to touch. It burned gold tonight. The imperfections were etched deeper than I was used to. Or perhaps I paid too little attention.

I could not have been in the garden for more than two full minutes before a shiver ran down my spine that had nothing to do with the cold. I made no effort to face him; there was no one else who could be behind me.

"You have told me that I should stay away from you. Yet here you are. Perhaps it is not I who is unable to stay away, Gabriel."

"So we are using Christian names now?"

I turned to flash him a look of irritation. His face was half illuminated in the light of the full moon, his brow drawn in frustration. He was quite skilled at evading my meaning. My use of his name was hardly the point of my little speech.

"We're alone in a moonlit garden. I rather think that what we call each other is the least improper thing about this situation."

"Does your perfectly respectable suitor know where you are? Who you are with?" His voice was low and grave with biting sarcasm.

It was ridiculous. I should be so lucky to have a husband like Lord Champaign. He would certainly make a better one than the man before me. But I knew the moment I stepped into the garden that Champaign and I would never wed. That he would have to make some other, better woman a very happy wife.

"You have made it clear that you have no interest in courting me. So why, exactly, are you so concerned with what my suitor does and does not know?" I asked.

"You know I cannot."

"Yes, you're an unrepentant rake," I said, as I tossed an eye roll in his direction. Just in case my opinion on that particular subject was unclear from my tone alone.

I continued, "You were eager to prove that at the theater. Well struck, by the way. You could not have chosen a demonstration more repulsive."

I moved to pass him, to return to the supper, brushing past his shoulder with feigned nonchalance.

He used the opportunity to catch my upper arm, to pull me back around to him. Just as I knew he would. His grip on my arm was tight, firm, unmistakable. I could probably pull free if I truly wished it. I had no desire to try.

"You needed to see." His voice had dropped half an octave to hang in the space between us.

"I saw quite clearly." I made a show of tugging against his grip. It was a half-hearted effort, but he released me. A sharp cold iced over the flesh abandoned by his hand.

"You know what I am. I've made no secret of it."

"Yes, and yet, who followed whom into the garden? You insist you're a rake. You are a seducer. I need to stay away from you. But you sought me out. Every single time. You watch me. So why are you trying to teach me the lesson? What do you want? Do you even know?"

"Of course I do, but I should not." His gaze flicked from my eyes and down to my lips, erasing any question of his meaning. "If I were to court you, you and I both know where it would end."

"What exactly do you call seeking me out? Dancing with me? If not the beginnings of a courtship. Your interest has been noted. It is far too late to warn me now. It was too late the moment you approached me in your mother's ballroom. We are already at the mountain's summit. Press forward or turn back, either way will only take us down."

"I do not seduce innocents. It is the only scrap of honor I possess."

He took a step back, his hands raised appealingly. My foot matched his and stepped forward without permission. His eyes widened slightly. A predatory shiver ran through me. I was not the prey here. He was.

A question was swirling in my mind, trapped on the tip of my tongue. Finally it dripped from my lips in a honeyed tone. "What if the innocent seduces you?"

"What?"

"You insist you are not like the other men of the *ton*. You are too clever and too worldly for my feminine tricks and wiles to affect you. And yet here you are, following me like all the others. In the end, that's all my game is—a seduction. I've seduced you." The words became truth as soon as I gave voice to them. Or perhaps they were always true.

"That is the most absurd—"

"I have. I've seduced you. Thoroughly. Completely. You are mine. Without reservation."

I took another hunting step toward him, but his feet were planted now. My eyes flitted over his form with hungry interest.

This was that brief, intoxicating moment of power when I walked away from him outside the theater, magnified a hundred-fold.

My toes met his, my head tipped back to maintain his gaze.

With heady, lusty delight, I spoke. "That is why, when I press my lips to yours in a moment, you are going to kiss me back. And when I undo your cravat, you will permit it. When I remove your waistcoat, you will assist me with the buttons. And so on. Until you are completely ruined for every woman who isn't me. Because you never had a choice in this matter. You have been mine since the moment you first set eyes on me. You simply did not know it yet."

He swallowed, his throat bobbing harshly with the effect of my words.

"Celine..." His voice graveled with what I could only describe as hunger.

"Close your eyes."

He did. And when I rose to my toes and met his lips with my own, he pressed back eagerly. His arm wrapped around my waist. Lifting me. Pulling me closer.

Surrendering to me.

Nine

LUCAS HOUSE, LONDON - MAY 28, 1807

JUST BECAUSE HE surrendered to the idea of me did not mean his lips acquiesced.

He kissed the way he did everything else. A dance. A battle. A sensuous, teasing push and pull. Grabbing me, maneuvering me to his liking.

Fortunately for him, I liked it too. Loved it, in fact.

I was rapidly losing the ground I had gained. His lips and his tongue and his hands stripping control from me, taking it for his own.

He broke away from my mouth to make his way down my jaw.

"You feel—" Words abandoned me too.

"What?"

"Gabriel…"

"Feeling less loquacious now?"

"Stop talking." I yanked him back down to my mouth. It seemed a particularly effective method of silencing him.

He was rapidly ripping away coherent thought. Vanquishing the desire for it as well. Who wanted to think when they could feel like this?

He tugged at the capped sleeve of my silk gown, freeing a shoulder for his lips. He could have the shoulder; he could have the rest of me as well. If his hands tugging blindly at the buttons lining the back of my gown were any indication, he was going to.

A pointed cough sounded from behind me, water dousing the fire to smolder.

Gabriel glanced up from his place buried in the hollow of my throat, biting out a bitter, ironic chuckle. I turned, straightening my gown as I did so.

Lord Champaign.

My stomach lurched with guilt. He did not deserve this treatment. Gentleman that he was, he even made an effort to politely avert his gaze while I righted myself.

"I wish to speak to Mademoiselle Cadieux for a moment. You are going to remain over there," he said, gesturing toward the other side of the veranda.

I forced myself to Lord Champaign's side, ignoring a grumble from Gabriel. "My lord, I—" I started with little idea of where I hoped to finish. It was a relief when he interrupted.

"Were you amenable to what I just saw?"

"I beg your pardon?"

"Were you amenable or did he force you?" His teeth gritted and his eyes darkened. The expression in no way resembled the amiable gentleman I had come to know.

But that question... How could he think such a thing?

"No! He would never."

Lord Champaign merely sighed and pinched the bridge of his nose. "Do you wish to marry him?"

"What?"

"Do you wish to marry him? It's a rather straightforward question given the circumstances."

"I don't—"

"You are compromised. You must marry," he interrupted again. "I may not have been the only one to see you. Do you wish to wed him?"

"I..."

"I would marry you if that was more to your liking. If we were engaged, I could offer you the protection of my name. My honor is unimpeachable. If I say we were out here together, then that is the truth," he said firmly.

"You would still?"

"Yes."

"I... I thank you for your incredibly generous offer, but I could not make you happy. You are far too kind to be satisfied with a wife such as myself."

"It is not a kindness. I like you very much. You are clever, funny, and lovely." He broke, grabbing one of my hands in his. "I know you do not have romantic feelings for me, Celine, but you find me less objectionable than other gentlemen. Marriages have been successful with far less as a foundation.

"However, if you would like to marry him... Well, I would question your sanity, but I would insist on it. You have no father or brother to force his hand. I could call him out."

"There is no need," Gabriel interjected from behind, his voice deathly cool with barely restrained ire.

"I was not speaking to you," Lord Champaign spat. His tone was something new, less affable than I'd ever heard from him.

"There is no need to call me out. And she will not be wedding *you*."

"It is not for you to decide. You will abide by her choice willingly, whatever it may be, or you will do so at the end of a blade."

Oh, good lord. That escalated quickly. Even men so well-mannered as Lord Champaign seemed to be incapable of having a conversation without resorting to violence. And they thought us the dramatic sex.

"She won't choose you. That's the point. She and I will wed, and your involvement is unnecessary and unwelcome."

"I would speak to him, privately, for a moment." I finally managed to get a word in between the two of them, gesturing toward Gabriel with my most hopeful doe eyes.

Lord Champaign sighed. It seemed I had overestimated my effect on him. I wondered in what other ways I had underestimated him.

"I will be over here. Chaperoning."

"Thank you." I grabbed Gabriel by the upper arm, tugging him back to the side of the veranda, manhandling him in his usual manner.

"Do you not think it a bit presumptuous to assert that we are to be wed without discussing it with me first?"

"What is there to discuss? You knew where this was headed."

"Well, yes, but I had not realized you did. I thought it would take another few weeks at least to get you to see the inevitability of it."

His gaze stormed over me. "You thought I would have you in my arms. Kiss you, taste you, love you, and be able to let you go?" He was utterly furious, his brows pinched and eyes narrowed. His hands came to grasp my forearms, gentle enough in spite of the irritation humming beneath the surface.

"Well, yes."

"And you thought to allow such a thing? Encourage it? Damn it all, Celine. You would infuriate Lucifer himself." He shook me, an emphasis really.

"Be more dramatic. Please," I snapped.

He released me abruptly. "Celine, I would not have given in if I did not intend to wed you. I told you, I do not seduce innocents."

"I thought we established that you were not the seducer."

"That is hardly the point."

"I rather think that is the point. You never would have allowed yourself to touch me if the choice were left to you."

"And so you sought to seduce me yourself. With the expectation that I would abandon you to face any potential consequences alone. Leaving you with nothing but hope that I would come to my senses and do the right thing?"

"I had not given it quite that much thought. I only had the idea a few moments ago."

"Enough. I cannot hear any more." Both hands came up to cup my cheeks, forcing a connection. "Are you going to marry me willingly or do I have to drag you down the aisle?"

Lord Champaign interrupted. "Rycliffe, she will not be dragged anywhere. She has options."

"No, she doesn't."

"Gabriel—" My tone was placating, an attempt to calm the tension in his form.

"Yes or no, Celine?"

"Yes." The word escaped me without thought or warning. Once it was free, it hung there between us. The single most important syllable I had ever uttered. And it felt so *right*.

"Very well. You have your answer, Champaign. You can run along now."

"I believe the two of you should head inside to announce your happy news. Don't you?" he replied with no hint of an option in his tone.

I chanced a glance behind me and saw that Lord Champaign was resigned. Disappointed but unsurprised. I wondered how much he knew before he set foot on the veranda. Whether any of this was a shock or if he had known all along that I was using him.

Before I could begin to utter any of the many apologies I owed him, Gabriel tugged me back around. He pressed a burning kiss to my lips before releasing me to follow along behind him.

To announce our engagement.

Giddy delight simmered—overtaking the guilt—bubbling under my feigned serenity.

Ten

MADEMOISELLE CADIEUX NO LONGER. I was Madame Hasket, Marquise of Rycliffe. A few words and I had a new home, new title, new role, new family, new name, new life. And a husband.

For such a momentous day, I did not feel particularly different. I wore my favorite gown, a hazy twilight-amethyst shade with bronze appliqué just below the bust and at the hem. A matching jeweled pin borrowed from Marie was tucked in my hair. Everything was pressed and styled with care.

Gabriel had been unaccountably quiet throughout the day, repeating as instructed, perhaps with more feeling than some grooms demonstrated, but not enough to be remarkable.

In honesty, he had taken on an even more mysterious air in the days since our engagement was announced. He procured a special license before eagerly leaving the rest of the planning to the purview of the ladies.

He had been unaccountably handsome this morning, though, in his dark coat and off-white cravat and waistcoat.

But he was inscrutable, even through the wedding break-fast. He watched me, as he always had, eyes heavy on my person, but he said as little as possible. I was becoming concerned with his interest in this marriage. He had seemed amenable enough, despite his hand having been forced, when the engagement was announced. But he'd paid no special attention to me in the week since. In fact, he had paid less attention than was appropriate. If he was so unhappy about the situation, would he not have allowed Champaign to wed me? Or at least encouraged me in that direction?

Seated at my new vanity, I traced a finger over the ring that now adorned my finger. Gold with a rose-cut diamond, it was far lovelier than anything I remembered of the jewels Mama and I had smuggled from France, but the scrollwork reminded me of her wedding ring slightly. I wondered if it was a family heirloom or if it was new. If there was a previous owner, she'd cared for it well. It was heavy on my finger, as it should be, a reminder of the vows I'd made today.

A knock echoed through my room, decorated in scrolls of creams and purples. It was lighter, airier, and more colorful than I'd expected, given the masculine decor of the rest of the house. Jane peeked her head in, offering her assistance with readying me for the night. I had been very studiously avoiding that thought and a small part of me cursed her for reminding me, but I nodded politely instead. It was hardly her fault that nerves had been building inside me for a week now. Ever since the ardor of the veranda had cooled.

She made her way behind me, brush in hand, before a cool, masculine voice interrupted.

"That will be all. I can see to Lady Rycliffe tonight." I hadn't even heard him enter.

Jane scurried off with a wide-eyed curtsy and not so much as a glance at me. Traitor.

"You will see to me, will you?" I watched in the mirror as he prowled from the adjoining room to tower over me. He'd stripped down to his shirt sleeves and cravat, though it was hanging loosely around his neck. His braces, too, hung uselessly about his thighs.

"I will."

"And what if that is not my wish?"

He bent down, aligning our faces, meeting my gaze in the reflection. "You swore to obey me today. I believe this falls under that promise."

My eye roll was mostly performance and his answering smirk was familiar, comforting. "I hardly think preventing my maid from seeing to me was part of that."

"It was. Now, these hairpins just pull loose?" He pulled up a nearby stool at my nod and began to pluck the decorative pins loose. Curl after curl fell free before he discovered the practical, hidden ones with a wordless noise of frustration.

"This is why you should have allowed Jane to assist me."

"Is it so wrong that I want to be the one to undress my wife on our wedding night?"

Oh... My heart flipped excitedly at the gravel in his tone and the heat in his eyes.

"Your wife?"

"I seem to recall you vowing something of the sort."

"I did, but you seemed less than enthused at the prospect this week." He caught my gaze in the glass again.

"Frustrated, were you?"

"Yes."

"I don't seduce innocents."

"I thought we established that I seduced you."

"Too bad we were interrupted by your pesky suitor. Now we'll never know..." The smirk deepened—infuriating man.

"No. I definitely seduced you," I insisted.

"Did you? Or did I merely allow you to think that?"

"You are an infuriating man."

"I know," he said, pressing a searing kiss to the back of my neck, just behind my ear. I felt it *everywhere*. "Now, I had planned to undo a few of these excessive buttons," he added, tapping a finger down the first few of the dozens lining my spine. "But if you would like to continue your seduction from the other night, I am more than willing for you to prove me wrong."

"I beg your pardon?"

"You insist you were the seducer the other night. Prove it." He stood abruptly and turned to the bed, and I spun on my stool to watch. He sat at the foot and leaned back on an arm with a challenging look in his eyes.

"You want me to..."

"Seduce me. Yes. You were certain you could manage it. I've never been seduced before, it sounds intriguing."

Whatever predatory, confident part of me took over the other night was nowhere to be found. In her place were nerves and far too many thoughts to silence. But I could not back down from his challenge, not with him sitting there entirely too smug.

I rose on shaky legs and went to stand before him. This would be slightly easier if I was already in my night dress, or better still, in nothing but a wrap. I was confident enough to know that the sight of my naked form would do the majority of the work for me.

But there were no less than five layers of fabric between us. And I could not possibly undo the line of buttons without his assistance. At least, not without pulling a vital muscle and appearing utterly ridiculous in the process.

Faced with the nerve-racking task of seducing my own husband, I considered the great number of places to begin. The majority of them were well outside the scope of Mama's vague and blush-filled "little talk." The longer I stood in front of him, desperately searching for an answer from the heavens, the more amused his smirk grew. Well, if I could not undress myself, perhaps undressing him would have a similar effect. Or inspiration would strike?

I knelt before him at the foot of the bed. His eyes widened with... surprise? Interest? I knew not where his thoughts lay. I forced myself to continue with my plan. I leaned forward to work the fastening of his boot.

He let out a breathy chuckle. My gaze shot back to his. "Was that wrong?"

His eyes fell shut and he shook his head, reaching out to cup my cheek in his hand.

"You can do no wrong, *ma amour*." The endearment resulted in both a heart flutter and a giggle. "What?"

"*Mon amour*."

"But you are a lady?" It was as I expected; he knew no French. But he had found the endearment. For me. I wondered if it was just that, an endearment. Or if he meant the sentiment behind it. *Love* was a word neither of us had approached. While I felt the possibility of it heavily, I did not yet know him well enough to assign the word to my feelings.

"It is the vowel... Do not worry about it," I answered distractedly, working on the other boot.

"But I looked it up."

"Do you really wish for a grammar lesson right now?" His eyes widened and he shook his head.

"No. Proceed with your seduction." He leaned back expectantly again. Perhaps I should have continued with the grammar. I was certain to do that correctly.

"Gabriel?" The trepidation was heavy in my voice but hopefully only perceptible to me.

"Yes?"

"Why did you laugh?"

"I did not expect you to remove my boot," he said, a grin clear in his voice.

"Oh... What did you expect?"

"Nothing." He leaned forward, dropping an elbow to his knee.

"No, you did. I saw it in your expression," I protested.

"Celine..."

"No, I want to do this properly."

His amused expression was well and truly gone now, replaced with something distressed, a pinching between the brows. I didn't know much, but I was certain a man was not supposed to wear that expression on his wedding night.

"As I said, there is no way to do this wrong." There was a sincerity in his tone and expression. He truly believed that. Now. Before he'd seen my pathetic attempts at this. Because whoever the seductress was that possessed me in that garden, she had well and truly forsaken me. My movements were stilted and awkward, nothing like the easy familiarity the woman in the theater had touched him with.

My response hovered at the tip of my tongue before spilling out all at once, words slurred together. "But I do not want you to be wishing you were with someone else."

"Why would you think that?"

"I am not experienced, like the woman in the theater. I do not know how to do what she does."

He pinched the bridge of his nose between thumb and forefinger with something like irritation. This was all wrong. The apologies were trapped beneath nerves. Marriage had made me a timid thing. I didn't know where this woman came from and I didn't like her—I missed the goddess on the veranda. I knew how to make men want me. I even know how to make Gabriel want me. But now, I was expected to do something with all that want. Why couldn't this have been intuitive the way the rest of it was?

His hand abandoned his nose and grabbed one of my shoulders while its companion found the other, pulling me to stand. That at least was familiar. Our vows did not include a clause to refrain from manhandling me. One hand left my shoulder and cupped my jaw, forcing my gaze to his.

"Celine, I won't insult your intelligence by lying to you. I've known women before. Too many." I tried to tug away, but the grip that remained on my shoulder tightened, preventing my escape. "Not once, not a single one of them, made me feel the way you do when you do nothing more than touch the fastening of my boot."

"But—"

"But nothing. I feel more for you when I watch you flirt with another man across a ballroom than I ever once did in another woman's bed. When I say that you can do no wrong, I mean it. I'm yours Celine. Do with me as you please. I will love it."

He leaned down and his hand caught my jaw while his lips found mine. He claimed first my upper lip, then broke away to make my lower lip his own.

I caught his bristled jaw in my palm, ensuring his mouth stayed pressed against mine, where it belonged while I stood, slotting into the space between his legs.

This—this was better. The spicy bergamot scent of my husband chased away the nerves, while his lips and hands chased away rational thought, until nothing was left but him.

He was overwhelming. The massive hand cupping my cheek spilled over onto my nape and jaw. It lit a spark inside me. His tongue demanded entrance to my lips. The symphony of heavy breaths, the slick slide of our mouths, the occasional whimper and more frequent groans filled the room, reaching a crescendo.

Gabriel set himself to the task of driving every last thought from my head. Nerves, modesty, and trepidation were the first to fall. He took and took and took. He took until only feeling, want, sensuality, and greedy delight were all that remained.

I caught the ends of his cravat in my hands, pulling him

closer. My efforts were met with a broken curse. Pleased with his reaction, I made a desperate tug at his shirt. He understood the meaning of my wordless yanking and tore free to rip it over his head before returning his lips to where they belonged. On me.

This time they fell to my jaw, then slid to my neck, my shoulder, my décolleté. His too big, too hot hand spanned the whole of my lower back, clutching me against him. The spark had become a fire and I only wanted to fan the flames higher. My hands, eager to touch that fire, to burn, wound in desperate, aimless patterns over his bare back. The nails of one hand digging into him, the other's fingers gripping his side.

My hand got caught in one of his braces. Not a hindrance, an asset. I grabbed and pulled, hard. Half the bedcovers came with his lower half when he rose to meet my hips. His lower half was proud and hard against me, just above where he would find a home inside me. Eager to see more, to feel more, my hands fell to the fastenings of his breeches.

His hands fell to mine, catching them on the second button with a breathy chuckle.

"My turn for a few minutes, wife."

"But... I am seducing you."

"And doing a damn fine job of it. But I want both of us to enjoy our wedding night." Weariness washed over me, cooling my ardor. Was he not—?

"Stop worrying," he whispered, pressing a kiss to my temple. "I meant you." His kiss dropped to my cheek. "If your present efforts are any indication, I suspect you will render me immobile and senseless for hours, if not days." His lips found my jaw. "I would like to ensure you are equally boneless and sated."

His hands released mine and found my waist, spanning it easily, his fingertips overlapping. He spun me around, still in the cradle of his thighs, to explore my back. There his lips found the vertebrae just above the cut of my gown. Heady anticipation danced down my spine. *That* was it. That was the feeling—the sensation—of his gaze. It was now so familiar and so delightful.

"Also, I do not know if you are aware, but I am a recently married man," he added. One dress button loosened with an audible *pop*. "And my wife... she is an exceptionally lovely woman." He freed the next button. "I have dreamed of her for months."

A third button and the dress began to gape. "I want to see her." Four. Kiss. Five. Kiss. Six. "All of her."

I was offered no respite. He moved immediately to my stays with ease. A flash of blonde hair and a low neckline whispered through my mind, gone as quickly as it had arrived when his lips found my neck. The structured fabric of my undergarments caught between us, no room to fall to the floor.

He nipped the nape of my neck gently, before soothing with his tongue and a desperate want settled between my thighs.

Unable to resist, I turned to him. My stays fell by the wayside until I was left in nothing but my gossamer shift. The fine fabric was impossibly thin and, if his groan was any indication, it offered little in the way of modesty. In fact, his breeches had all but abandoned their futile effort to hide him from my gaze as his length projected with interest.

Gabriel lighting a trail of need along the neckline of my shift with a single finger before catching the tiny bow nestled between my breasts. He tugged it playfully before flicking his intense dark gaze to mine with a raised brow.

"Yes," I said, darting a tongue out to wet my suddenly dry lips. He caught the end of the ribbon between his thumb and forefinger. A sharp tug and I was bare before him.

A groan of my name escaped him, and, oh, I wanted him

to say my name like that *always*. As though it were the beginning and end of his vocabulary. As if I were his only thought.

The way his eyes slid along my frame, lingering on my breasts, the place between my thighs—I wanted him to look at me that way always too. Soft. Hot. Overcome.

His hand hovered questioningly above my waist. I caught it in my own and pulled it to one breast where I pressed it home.

"Fuck, Celine."

I didn't need to ask if that was a good curse. I knew. Everything here was perfect.

His fingers worked my nipple, first testing the motions before finding the one where my head fell back with a curse of my own. His free hand spanned my back, bringing me closer to him. His mouth found the lonesome breast and lavished it with attention.

This time when my hands found the fastening on his breeches he made no protest. I finished undoing the buttons, and he lifted his hips off the bed to assist, though his efforts were half-hearted. He was chiefly occupied with mapping my body with his lips and fingers.

Then one of those deft fingers found the cleft between my legs... I was not entirely ignorant of the pleasure to be found there, but his fingers, his touch... He read my body in a way I had not managed on my own. One finger found my entrance, then two. His thumb found the magical place just in front, a spot that turned the flames inside me into a bonfire.

I forgot all words that weren't his name. Then I forgot that, too, and was left with nothing but desperate, wordless cries until I could do nothing but fall apart in his arms. Ash, burned by his inferno.

His hand on my waist was all that kept me upright until I regained control of my limbs. The other hand, the one I wanted to write sonnets about, was working his shaft with a fervor.

"Gabriel?" His name remained the only speech I was capable of at the moment.

"Hmm?"

"Can you...? Was that...? Is that...?"

"I've finally rendered you senseless," he whispered with a smirk that was more charming than infuriating. "I'm quite proud of that."

"Can I...?" I gestured to where his hand was working on his person.

"Touch my cock?"

"Is that what you call it?"

"One of many names. My preferred."

"Can I touch your cock?" My tentative question earned a groan as his eyes fell shut in abandon.

"You're trying to kill me. As I said, you can do whatever you like with me. I'm yours."

He ceased his efforts when I reached out an uncertain hand and brushed my fingers over the impossibly soft skin of his hard member. He was even hotter there—if that was possible. Wrapping my hand around his cock, I tried to replicate his motions.

He caught my mouth in a heated kiss, breaking away only to whisper, "You can... harder. If you'd like."

In response I tightened my grip and earned another groan. After a few moments I managed to copy the rhythm he'd used and his hips joined the effort.

He only allowed our shared dance for a moment before pulling away with a curse. My confusion must have been written on my face because he offered a brief kiss before answering my unasked question.

"I need to be inside you now. Tell me you need it too."

"*Yes*." My response slipped free in a breathy rush.

He dipped a hand between my legs again, playing his palm and fingers over my entrance gently with purpose. My hips chased his hand of their own accord when he pulled away.

"You are ready, aren't you?" He grinned. "Tell me, did you ever picture us together? How did you imagine it?"

"I don't..."

He grabbed my waist and hauled me up onto the bed over him, one of my knees on each side of his hips. The position left me hovering over his cock.

"Did you imagine taking me inside you like this?" He thrust his hips up to erase the nonexistent doubt as to his meaning. "Were we lying beside each other? Did you ride me?"

"You were over me, surrounding me, everything I could see and hear and feel was you." And *oh*, how I wanted that. I wanted him and me together until there was nothing else left.

"You make me doing all the work sound incredibly romantic."

"But..."

"It's all right. You can do the work next time." He added a cheeky, crooked grin to ensure I took his meaning. Then he hauled me farther up the bed, dropping me in a nest of too many pillows, arranging himself to suit my fantasies.

He was propped on his elbows above me, and it was everything I wanted. Gabriel and only Gabriel.

"You must tell me if I hurt you. If you change your mind or don't like something. If I should do something differently. And especially, especially tell me if I do something that feels good." His grin deepened, but his eyes held nothing but sincerity.

At my nod, he pressed forward. His entry was slow and gentle. It felt, if not precisely good, intriguing. His brow pinched with concentration and, after a moment, his hips met mine. His breath was ragged in the space between us.

Tentatively, testing, I wrapped one leg around his waist,

and he somehow slipped deeper inside me. He seemed to take my adjustment as tacit permission to retreat and advance again, twisting his hips on the exit and re-entry.

Interesting became good and then incredible in short measure.

Groans of "yes," "more," and "don't stop," escaped without permission. My hands were restless and desperate on his back, chest, bottom; clutching, digging, dragging. Once-gentle thrusts became sharper and so did the pleasure they gave.

Pants of my name, curses wrapped in groans, and unintelligible moans overtook him just as the inferno overtook me. Lost and burning in the dancing flames, I was only dimly aware when he followed me moments later.

It was some minutes before he gathered the strength to roll to the side, bringing me along to nestle on top of him. He pressed a kiss to the top of my head while I settled into a more comfortable position, bundled against his side.

Gradually, our breathing evened out while he combed his fingers through my hair with affection.

"So," he broke the silence. "I have to agree. You have thoroughly and completely seduced me."

I bit back a smile. "Yes, I've ruined you for anyone else."

"Quite right." Silence followed for a beat before a chuckle escaped him and my giggle joined the song.

Pleasure and humor in one man. I had made an excellent choice in husband.

Eleven

"SUCH A PROVIDER..." I murmured from my cocoon among the bedcovers several hours and little deaths later. My husband, his arms ladened with the remnants of our wedding breakfast, rolled his eyes and shut the door behind him.

"If you're going to mock, I won't be sharing."

"Who was mocking? I would never mock a man in possession of cake, and is that cheese?"

"It is, and the closest thing we had to a French loaf. I know it will pale in comparison to your refined palate." He settled his feast onto the bed, climbing up after it.

"Do you know, I don't actually remember what *real* bread tastes like. Mama and Marie always say it is lacking here. They would know better than I."

He spread a bit of butter on the bread before topping it with a piece of cheese and passing it to me.

"It has been a number of years for me, but our cook does a credible job of it from what I remember," he explained between bites of his own.

"I shall have to take your word for it," I said, licking a

butter-covered finger. When I met his ochre gaze, the sincere interest was clear. "Can I tell you a secret?"

"Always."

"There is much of France I do not remember. Even my accent has become somewhat forced," I said sheepishly.

"I know."

"How could you possibly know?" Nothing could have kept the snappish irritation from my voice.

"It slips when you are infuriated. Or aroused." He grinned conspiratorially.

"It does not!"

"It does. Do not worry, though. I am the only one who infuriates you. And I certainly plan to be the only one to arouse you."

"You are a menace," I whined. "I have lived two-thirds of my life in this country. I was but a girl when we left."

"We could go for a visit if you'd like. Once tensions have eased."

"I would adore that." I could see it clearly in my mind, Gabriel feeding me bites of croissant while I was wrapped indulgently in the bedcovers with the music of Parisian streets curling around us through the open window.

He held out a forkful of cake for me to taste. The burst of currants and the floral-oaken flavor of the brandy melted on my tongue.

Seemingly pleased with my response, he offered me another bite, this one with more icing on it. Though beautiful, I found the icing too sweet for my palate. I shook my head.

"Too much icing?" I nodded and he ate that bite, returning with one that was entirely cake. "You wrinkle your nose when something is too sweet. Did you know that?"

"How is it that we've been married less than a day, and you know all my secrets?"

"I watched you."

"I've been wondering about that. How long? I first felt someone watching me at the Cavendish Party... A year past, or nine months perhaps?"

"A few months before that, maybe. It wasn't anything particularly eventful. You and your mother were calling on my mother. You walked down the stone steps with a little smile. You didn't have your bonnet on." He caught a curl and tugged on it before releasing it. "The sun caught on your hair and you had this *glow* about you. I had never seen anything like it."

With a finger, he traced the lines of my cheek and jaw. "I dismissed such sentimental nonsense, of course. A trick of the light. You were a lady far too innocent for the likes of me."

"It was almost certainly a trick of the light. And not so—"

"But then I saw you holding court at the Cavendish party, the entire *ton* fawning over this little slip of a lady. Begging for your attentions... Hanging on your every word... And I realized it was you—just you."

"You know so much of me, and I know next to nothing about you. You were determined to remain mysterious. Tell me something."

"What do you wish to know?"

"Anything—everything. Something I do not know."

He popped a bit of bread in his mouth and chewed with a thoughtful expression. Then, he settled back against the pillows, guiding me to rest my cheek against his heart. Wrapping another one of my disheveled curls around his finger, he studied it with far more attention than it was due. "Your hair... it's softer than spun silk."

"You, husband, are avoiding the question."

He answered with little more than a resigned sigh. He made a valiant effort to distract me with another piece of cheese. Under usual circumstances it would have been an effective tactic, but I was determined to know him.

I shook my head, dismissing the cheese.

"Must we? We have our entire lives to learn about each other. I would rather not spoil tonight."

"You seem to be laboring under the misapprehension that I have no idea who I married. I did witness your little show with your... *friend* at the theater. I am aware that you will not be nominated for sainthood. I was not asking for a confessional. Just something new."

He sighed again, catching his glass of brandy from the side table. "That was poorly done, I'll admit. Very well... I enjoy the races, sometimes. Shooting and fencing as well."

"Such masculine pursuits. Do you suppose you could teach me to fence? It has always interested me."

He choked on a sip of the brandy. "You wish to learn to fence?"

"The request was primarily in jest. But it was not a lie. I do wish to learn. It was fascinating when my brother was learning."

Gabriel studied me thoughtfully for a moment, sizing me from toes to nose. "I would need to commission a sword for you. Mine are too unwieldy for someone your size."

"You would teach me? Truly?"

"If you wish to learn. Though, it might be best to hire an instructor. I am not known for my teaching skills."

It was my turn to study him. With a raised brow, I surveyed the man before me. Hair bedraggled, scores down his shoulders from my nails, a love bite on his neck—he was perfect.

"You were a more than passable teacher this evening."

"Passable! Passable? That was a revelation and you know it, wife."

I could not restrain the pleased hum that escaped me at yet another mention of my new title.

"It was unobjectionable," I teased.

Of course, he was well aware that his touch left me desperate. His crooked smirk made that perfectly clear.

His silky eyes glided along my bare form. There was little question that I was just as marked and well-loved as him, perhaps more so.

He pulled my lips to his with one firm, oversize hand cupping my cheek, jaw, nape.

Drawing away for a breath he muttered, "I will show you unobjectionable."

"Please do..."

Twelve

RYCLIFFE PLACE, LONDON - AUGUST 30, 1807

IT SHOULDN'T HAVE COME as a surprise. As often as there were seven- and eight-month babies in the *ton*, there was an equal number of ladies who took months, even years, to conceive. But the familiar, entirely unpleasant sensation that marked the beginning of *that time* that came midnote at the pianoforte still shook me.

If Davina noticed when I faltered, she gave no indication of it. Though, as usual, she wasn't particularly interested in her music lessons. I could hardly blame her. I wasn't anything like qualified to teach. But she'd chased off another governess last week and I'd volunteered in a desperate attempt to prevent the inevitable bloodshed should Her Grace take up the mantle. Every day since, she'd been deposited at my doorstep for her lessons.

Unfortunately, I hadn't accounted for this type of bloodshed. "Excuse me," I whispered, slipping from the room without explanation. I managed the halls as swiftly as I could without drawing attention, then finally pressed my back against the door to the rooms Gabriel and I shared.

Even though I knew what I'd find when I tugged up the

layers of skirts, something inside my belly still dropped when I felt the familiar dampness of my chemise and pulled my hand away to find a smear of red.

I'd been prepared. Four weeks ago, I had made my regular preparations at the usual time. I hadn't even allowed the thought for another sennight, after which it became impossible to keep my suspicions at bay.

But each morning with no familiar staining on my chemise gave rise to expectations, to hope. All of which had just been dashed by a single soiled strip of linen. I swallowed back the swirl of sentiment rising in my throat before pulling the bell. I quite liked the lace on this chemise and Jane would need to work quickly if it was to be salvaged.

The petite maid arrived quickly and with a sharp knock, unused to my summons at this time of day.

"How can I help you, madam?" she asked when I opened the door.

"I need to change. A new chemise, if you please."

The girl blinked slowly at me for a moment before jumping into action when comprehension dawned. "Oh dear, of course. Right away."

"This one will need to be laundered today."

"Yes, yes," she answered, pulling a chemise from the chest of drawers and my other necessities from a trunk by my toilette before coming around to my back to make short work of the buttons, petticoats, stays, and stained chemise without comment.

Once I was settled into my chemise, she asked, "Do you need help with your dress?"

"No, thank you. I'd like to rest. If you could call for the carriage and let Lady Davina know I have a headache and she is released from lessons for the day, it would be most appreciated."

"Right away. And we can treat this stain quickly. I should be able to salvage it."

"Thank you," I replied, settling before my vanity while she plucked the pins from my hair and twisted it into a simple braid before tying it off with a worn ribbon.

"Madame, if it's not too bold to say, I am mightily sorry. I'm sure you were feeling hopeful."

Snappish bitterness and gratitude for her kindness fought for dominance. In the end I settled for a nod, not willing to scold her for her speculation. It was to be expected when I wed the heir to a dukedom.

Oppressive silence settled over the room when I crawled into the oversize bed. It was too large and too cold without Gabriel's large frame to fill it. I curled onto my side and refused to let the tears I could feel building behind my eyes take form. There hadn't been a babe to mourn. This was an absurd overreaction to a normal function.

Time was impossible to track here in the darkened room while I stared at the dent in Gabriel's pillow. It wasn't even from his head. It was probably just over-fluffed.

Some indeterminate minutes, hours, days later, I heard the door open and close behind me. The only indication that it wasn't Jane with a hot-water bottle or herbal tea was the return of the burdensome silence and my usual awareness of Gabriel.

When I felt the edge of the bed dip behind me and a solid arm wrapped around my waist while the other slipped under the divot between my head and shoulder, it wasn't a surprise. Then his warmth tucked along my back. Wordlessly, Gabriel dropped a kiss to my jawline and tightened his hold. His breath danced along the back of my neck when he pressed his forehead there.

My next inhalation was thick and ragged, entirely without permission. Gabriel's only response was to tighten his arms further still. Tracing his forearm from the rolled edge of his sleeve to his hand, I laced my fingers through his. He squeezed back, his breath steady and sure against me.

It wasn't until the tear slipped down my nose to hang there for a second before spilling onto the hand I had curled beneath my cheek that I realized they'd finally made their escape. I flicked it away with my free hand, irritated with my own silliness.

"Cee..." The word brushed along my spine.

"It's nothing," I replied, except my voice was tight and too high-pitched for it to truly be nothing.

"It's not nothing."

"No, it is. My courses were late, that is all."

His chest rose and fell, but something was tight and staccato in the sensation along my spine. "And we both thought it might be something."

"You knew?"

"I suspected. I can count, you know." There was the lightest tease in the words, and that was a comforting balm.

"I'm sorry. I wanted to be—for you."

He stiffened against me before relaxing again. "Just for me?"

"For everyone. They're all waiting and wondering, you know."

"Bugger everyone else, Celine. I care about you," he growled into my neck. "What did—do—you want?"

"You need an heir."

"'S what Xander is for."

"But—"

"I need *you*," he insisted, turning me to face him. His dark eyes roved my face, surely splotched and pale. Whatever he saw there had him slamming his lips against mine. It wasn't a kiss to arouse, to entice. It wasn't gentle or romantic. It was a frantic plea for something I couldn't name.

Just as suddenly as it began, he broke it off and continued. "My father—the rest of the world—can hang. What I need to know is what do *you* want. Not what you think I want. Not what you know everyone else wants."

My fingers found the furrow of his brow, smoothing it away without conscious permission. "I—" I broke off, swallowing the overwhelm of him, of this situation, of my new life as a future duchess, of the responsibilities that entailed. "I think we would make beautiful babies. Our children would bring the *ton* to its knees. And I want to meet them... Someday."

"Not today?"

I shook my head. "I wouldn't be saddened if it were to happen. But... no. I'm not ready just yet."

"All right," he said, trailing delicate fingers along my shoulder, tracing the neckline of my chemise.

"What *do* you want?"

He hummed and pressed his lips on my forehead. "I would think a lady such as yourself, so skilled at reading men, would know what I want."

The obvious answer sprang to mind. "But surely not while..."

He chuckled, his lip curling at the corner. "Not tonight, though I like that thought. No, right now, I'd like to hold you for a while. And then I'd like to feed you. Then, if it's quite all right with you, I think I'll hold you again."

That sounded like perfection itself. Except for one needling thought.

"You didn't answer me though."

He sighed and tucked my head into the crook of his neck. His fingers brushed the loose curls from my crown back behind my ear.

"You're quite right. Our children would run the world. But I like having you to myself, for now at least."

"So, someday."

"Yes, but not today," he murmured, the vibrations of his chest soothing against my chest. "After all, we have the rest of our lives."

"We do," I agreed, drifting off to the steady drum of his heartbeat.

Thirteen

RYCLIFFE PLACE, LONDON - SEPTEMBER 25, 1807

"THIS ONE, I THINK." Davina gestured to the delicate amethyst pendant resting on my chest of drawers. It was one of more than a few glittering gifts from my husband.

At three and ten, my new sister was already more fashionable than most of the *ton*. And somewhat less eccentric in her choices than her equally fashionable mother. I held the pendant to my throat and turned to her for approval.

She nodded enthusiastically and I agreed. It would serve quite well for a burst of color against the shimmering gold of my gown. Only a shade or two darker than my natural golden complexion, the dress did require the embellishment of accessories.

A brisk knock on the door signaled a visitor—not Gabriel. He never knocked on the door to our chambers at home. Xander peeked his head in after I bade entry.

Gabriel's younger brother was all nerves tonight. The mere thought of his first society ball had turned him a putrid shade of yellowing green.

"Gabe is going to be late. He sent a note that he will meet us there," Xander said in a half sigh.

I bit back the instinctive irritation at that intelligence. "Is anything the matter?"

"He does not say."

He never said. He was merely late to the dinner, ball, or garden party. Or missed it entirely.

"Very well." With a forced smile, I continued. "I do not suppose there is a gentleman here who would be able to accompany me for the first set? Since my husband is not here to request it."

Xander's eager gaze shot to mine. "Oh, please, Cee? It would make the whole evening so much easier."

"I would be honored to dance with you, Monsieur Hasket. You look very fine tonight." And he did.

Unlike his sister, Xander had not adopted a color palette and instead followed in his mother's *monochromatique* footsteps. The excess of black made him appear older and more imposing than his twenty years and second-son status dictated. Neither a grandiose presence or severe countenance would dissuade the desperate ladies or the machinations of their mamas.

I worried for him. My suspicions were just that, but I worried there was not a single lady in the whole of England who could tempt him. And I worried that more than one gentleman would.

Such things were verboten here. Though not strictly encouraged in the French Court, they were more accepted. Perhaps I could convince Gabriel to allow him to join us on our promised trip to the continent.

If he ever returned home, that was.

Something had changed in him after that day when my briefest hope vanished. It sparked something in Gabriel. Suddenly, he had engagements, meetings, dealings at all hours of the day—and occasionally the night. It had been some weeks since he'd returned to whatever mysterious activities he enjoyed before our marriage. The distracting kisses and evasive caresses had begun to wear thin and tonight was only the latest in a string of late arrivals.

But tonight, it was particularly upsetting. Not for me, but for his brother.

Just that morning, I expressed the need for him to be prompt. His presence would help soothe Xander's nerves. No matter how supportive, I was no replacement for an elder brother. Now Gabriel was so late he would not even arrive before our departure.

This was certainly a downside to a husband who was, at least in part, immune to my charms. Ellsworth would have been home on time; I had no doubt of that. Lord Champaign, too, never would have insulted me so. Nor any of the others. What had seemed dull mere months ago shone in a new light.

Still, none of my musings would calm Xander's nerves tonight. I rose to the dressing table—more abruptly than intended if the siblings' startle was any indication. Shifting through the clutter on Gabriel's table, I managed to find the pocket watch I had in mind.

"Here. This would suit rather well, I think," I said, handing it to the greenish boy.

Davina, sensing her brother's discomfiture, proceeded as Davina was wont to do. "You look very handsome tonight, Xander. You must tell me absolutely everything! Do you think you will find a wife tonight? What if you spill lemonade on her? Or what if you meet a lady and she is supposed to be your wife, but you trod on her foot? I would never marry anyone who did that to me."

The girl had been firing questions at her brother rapidly all day, each driving him further into his panic than the last. While I usually found their needling dynamic amusing, tonight I could not condone it.

"Davina, your brother is far too young for marriage to any

young lady. He needn't worry about the repercussions of trodden feet or spilled drinks until he is much older."

"But surely people *talk*. When it is time for him to marry, they will remember that he bungled tonight up."

"Certainly not. Someone will do something scandalous by the end of the week that will be infinitely more interesting than any misstep Xander could make. Not that he will make any."

Xander paused in his determination to wear a hole straight through my floorboards to offer me a grateful smile.

"Now, shall we be off? I believe I promised my first set to the most handsome gentleman of my acquaintance, and I shan't be late for it."

~

XANDER MANAGED NOT one but two dances and only trod on my toe once. And, still, his brother remained elsewhere.

The younger Hasket now hovered awkwardly on the outside of a circle of gentlemen. He strove to look as though he were part of the conversation but received absolutely no acknowledgment.

Gabriel would not likely survive the tongue lashing I was preparing.

Out of the corner of my eye, I caught a glimpse of a blonde head far above the rest—Lord Champaign. He would help Xander, I was certain of it. But how to summon him? I was married now. I could not simply bat my eyelashes his way with a coy smile and a brush of my fan across my bosom. I filed through my repertoire for something—anything—to attract his attention without forsaking my marriage vows. Nothing.

I scanned the crowd for another option, perhaps someone

already focused on me. None was forthcoming. No longing gazes were cast in my direction. No preening gestures were performed for my interest.

It was gone.

I was invisible.

I'd traded my only currency for a wedding ring. And the husband that came with it was nowhere to be found.

Suddenly, it had become very lonely on the edge of this dance floor. I was alone here, surrounded by gentlemen who once courted my favor as though it was the greatest gift anyone could bestow.

Marquise, someday to be a *duchess*.

And I may as well have been a speck of dust on the floor for all the interest it garnered. Had flirting been my life's purpose? Was that all the *ton* thought me good for?

I glanced toward the wallflowers. I recognized a few of them, but none I would consider friends. My closest ally was Xander, and he was still standing pathetically just outside a circle of gentlemen. What use was I to him?

From across the room came a bright feminine laugh. Ellsworth, Parker, Westfield, James, Ashfield—they all gathered around her.

A blonde head, no taller than my own, was thrown back as she tapped Ellsworth's arm with her fan just so. He flushed and stammered, just as he always had when I'd made the same move.

Each and every one of the boobies of the *ton* clamored for her attention. And then she turned to me.

The floor dropped out from under my feet.

The lady from the theater.

The smirk she favored me with was knowing, self-satisfied, drifting into something vaguely sinister before she turned back to her admirers. From this distance, my impression of her was much clearer than it had been from across the entire theater. Her hair was bright and golden, like mine. Perhaps her complexion was a bit paler—more fashionable, really. Our height and build were almost identical.

I could barely make out her words from across the ballroom, but I may have detected a hint of a French accent. It was slightly less authentic than my own, but nothing the *ton* would detect.

She was me. A newer, unwed version of me.

And, if my understanding of the events in that theater box was correct, a much more adventurous version as well.

I had been used, discarded, and now I was worthless to the *ton*.

And that *woman* had enjoyed my husband's attentions, carnally. Perhaps for years. Was she the one to teach him the pleasures he demonstrated on my person night after night? I could not retain the bitter chuckle that thought brought forth. If that were the case, I should thank her.

I sensed his presence mere seconds before his words brushed my ear. "What, pray tell, is so amusing?" His voice was thick and sweet like honey, but it was paired with the cloying scent of differing liquors and too many cigars. Ice ran through my veins at the sight of him, rather than the usual smoldering heat.

The words broke free before I could grasp them. Before I could remind myself that men do not enjoy bitter, nagging women. "I was just thinking that I should thank your friend over there. She is the one responsible for your prowess, is she not?"

"I beg your pardon?" Gone was the honey, and in its place honed steel.

I turned to meet his gaze finally. His brow was furrowed, and his body curved over me. Intimidating rather than intriguing for possibly the first time. His feigned ignorance was enough to light a different fire than I was used to. Anger, rather than lust, fueled the set of my shoulders and jut of my chin.

"Your friend, the one who allowed your hand up her skirts in the Theatre Royale. I presume she is the one who taught you to use your hands? Mouth too, I suppose? I should thank her. After all, our marriage exists solely between the sheets, so at least she has ensured that is an enjoyable prospect." Though the words were hissed, they were far too loud for our present location.

Yet I could not have stopped myself from continuing for anything, not now.

"I could not help but notice the resemblance. Clearly you have preferences. I suppose I should count myself fortunate to meet them."

His hand engulfed my upper arm, tight, harsh, as he pulled me as subtly as he could out of the ballroom and into the hall. Once free of the cloying, muggy ballroom, with slightly fewer prying eyes, he was less subtle. Gabriel tugged me down one corridor, then another, opening and closing doors at random.

Finally, he found an empty study. He all but shoved me in, slamming the door behind us.

"Would you care to tell me what in the damned hell has gotten into you?"

"Nothing has gotten into me!"

"I beg to differ. What is it you're talking about with Victoria?"

"Victoria? Is that her name? Lovely. I noticed that the two of you arrived at nearly the same time. I presume she is the reason you were late?"

"What? Of course not. I haven't seen her in months. Since that night at the theater." There was no lie in his eyes. Fury— yes, but lies—no. But I had come too far to stand down.

"Oh, of course. You gave up your mistress months ago. How silly of me. You disappear all hours of the day and night with no explanation because you are off what? Playing croquette? You come back smelling of a distillery and ladies' perfume because you're attending art classes? Is that the story I am to believe?"

"You knew what I was when you married me. I have never claimed to be anything other than what I am."

"You have told me nothing! Every time I ask anything you change the subject, or you distract me with kisses."

"Damn it all, Celine! You do not need to know." His hands wrenched in front of him, seemingly aiming to shake me, though he closed no distance.

"Of course. I do not need to know anything. It's not as though I'm your wife."

"Celine..." The word was an exasperated sigh as he raked a hand through his hair.

"No, no, Gabriel. I have given up everything to be your wife, and you will not even tell me where you spend your time."

"What do you mean you've given up everything?"

"Look at me! I'm nothing. A pretty, broken bauble, all but useless on a shelf. I used to be the jewel of the *ton*. Now, no one will even look at me except your smirking mistress. My husband spends his days and nights elsewhere, doing Lord knows what. And I am left to stand on the edge of a dance floor alone and watch the same people that used to idolize me ignore me. I should have wed Champaign. At least he would not have abandoned me."

"Don't you ever say that again," he bit through gritted teeth.

"What? That I am useless? That you're off whoring about? That I should have listened to you and married anyone else?"

"Any of it! All of it!" It was the first time he'd raised his voice in the entire exchange and it startled me slightly.

"Why not? It's the truth."

"Of course it's not! And I swear if you mention Champaign one more time it shall be pistols at dawn!"

"That is what you took from all I said?"

"Celine... You're not useless, you're perfect." His tone and expression returned to the quiet fury, but the words doused the fire inside me to a simmer. "But honestly, of course they won't so much as look at you. You're mine, and they're terrified of me. Rightly so, I might add. A fact you might wish to take note of at some point."

"Oh please, you're not going to hurt me. You desire nothing more than to strangle me right now, and you're still halfway across the room." I gestured at the still-significant distance between us. The certainty with which that statement escaped me was surprising, but it was true. Even pulling me from the ballroom, he had been careful not to injure me. Though my arm still burned from his touch, it wasn't a physical pain.

"You're wrong," he ground out.

"What?"

"There's one thing I wish to do more than strangle you." His eyes darkened with something other than fury, and my body reacted as usual and entirely without permission. But I was not finished with him.

"Gabriel, you may wish for something else, but I *do* wish to strangle you!"

"Cee... this is not the place. We'll discuss this at home."

"You're never at home, and when you are, you just drag me off to your bed."

"Did you wish me to drag you elsewhere?" His smirk shifted to something crooked and confident. He was wearing me down. He knew it, and it pleased him.

"Gabriel!"

"Celine, there is no one else. I have not touched another woman since that night at the theater. And really, that entire display was to put you off, quite the success story. If you believe nothing else, surely you must believe that. I hardly have the stamina to keep a woman on the side. You're far too demanding a lover."

He raised a brow, slipping his gaze from my toes to my curls. As always, I felt it—a tangible thing—burning touch through every layer of fabric.

Gabriel continued, "Too beautiful too. How could anyone look at you and consider anyone else?"

"Gabriel..." He took a tentative step forward, testing the waters. When I made no move to back away, he closed the gap and wrapped both hands around my upper arms, searing me. Closer now, without the surrounding ballroom, I could still smell the liquor and cigars but none of the ladies' perfume from before. He was not lying about that at least.

Releasing one arm to tip my chin to force my eyes to his, he searched my face for something.

I didn't know what he found there, but his lids shuttered against it and his forehead met mine. The gesture was enough for all of my anger and most of my hurt to abandon me.

"Celine, let's go home."

"It's your brother's first ball. He's probably still trying to get someone to talk to him."

"And I forgot..." he added with a frustrated nod of under-standing.

"And you forgot. I was trying to find someone to talk to him, but no one would look at me." My voice was small and weak, and I hated it just a little.

"And then everyone was looking at Victoria..."

"I detest that name."

"Of course."

"I mean it."

"I believe you. We won't name any of our children Victoria. Let us go find my brother and see if we can escape without any more theatrics. We can talk at home."

"Promise?"

"Promise." He sealed it with a warm kiss to my forehead.

Fourteen

POOR XANDER RELEASED a visible sigh of relief when his brother nodded sharply toward the door. He was still trapped on the periphery of the ballroom and had made no obvious progress in our absence.

The ride back to the house after dropping Xander off at home was quiet save for the steady patter of rainfall that had begun sometime while we were in the ball. The air was filled with a thick quiet, full of unspoken discontent hanging heavy and waiting for release.

My earlier outrage was reduced to a simmer, but it remained, bubbling underneath the surface, swirling with infuriating hints of lust. The streets passed in an indistinguishable blur of lamplight and raindrops out the window of the carriage.

Our arrival at Rycliffe Place was clearly a surprise to the staff who were, for the first time in my residence, unprepared for our return. I dismissed Jane with a worry that I would regret that decision after my discussion with my husband.

Gabriel made the wise choice not to dawdle and his sharp knock at my dressing-room door arrived swiftly.

I opened it to find him leaning against the wall across the hall, eyeing me with interest.

"Don't you dare try to seduce me. You promised, and I'm still cross with you," I snapped.

A weary sigh escaped as he trudged to the settee and collapsed on it. His elbows found his knees, and his head rested heavily in his hands.

He was a large man, my husband, but in that moment he looked small, weak. It was a side of him I had never seen before. I did not like it. That I was the cause of such an expression... well, that caused a sharp, painful kick just under my rib —to my heart.

"What do you wish to know?" His question was directed toward the carpeting, the plush lavender rug I'd added a mere week ago.

Questions churned through me, stored for weeks, for months. I settled into the chair across from him before I addressed the most serious of my wounds.

"I suppose I should start with her. You said her name was Victoria?"

"Yes, or that is her chosen name."

"Do you know her real name?"

"Yes."

"So you are confidants." It was a statement more than a question.

"We were. For many years."

"How many years?"

"Four, maybe five? I do not know exactly."

"And she is a... professional?"

"Yes."

"Do I need to be concerned for my health?" His gaze shot up, eyes wide and brow furrowed.

"No! Of course not. Victoria and I had an... exclusive arrangement."

"So, she is the only one?" I asked tentatively. Then I steeled myself for the impact of his answer.

"Only one in years. I have always been careful."

"Are there children?" I braced against that potential blow as well.

"What?"

"Do you have illegitimate children?"

He paused, eyes slipping closed and head slipping back to his hands.

I knew then the answer would not please me. My stomach churned at that thought.

"I do not know. There are none that I am aware of."

"What would you do if one came forward?"

"What would I do if—" He broke off with a sigh. "I suppose provide for them, set them up with an education or dower them as appropriate." That response was directed back at my carpet.

"How did your relationship with Victoria begin?"

"I do not know, Celine..." His head tipped back against the settee, his gaze firmly on the ceiling. "I was young and foolish, running up gambling debts, and enjoying the company of married women. I created more than a few enemies. And I spent too much time and too much money at the brothel she worked in. It was a terrible place. Truly. There were women there. I wasn't very particular then. But she was a favorite and apparently it was mutual. One night, after— We got to talking. I was complaining about one of the gentlemen I had made an enemy of... and she told me a few of his secrets. Something to get him off my tail.

"She learned a lot of secrets in her profession. Instead of dismissing her, I recognized that her knowledge could be useful."

Gabriel's heavy hand dragged through his hair, ending at his neck. There he rubbed at a knot in his shoulder. "She wanted more in life. I helped her out of that brothel and became an investor in hers. She runs a tight ship, takes care of her girls. We began an exclusive relationship that lasted until that night. At the theater."

"What was she doing at the Rutlidge ball tonight?"

He righted his head. His eyes, darkened to charcoal, met mine again. "Searching for another paramour, I suspect. Lord Rutlidge is a patron of her establishment, I believe. He likely convinced his wife to invite her as a distant cousin or some such nonsense."

"Those gentlemen, they were trying to curry her favor?"

"Her paramour is one of the most powerful men in London. As the madame of the most exclusive and popular brothel, she knows everything that happens in this city. The man in her good graces? Well, there is little he cannot achieve." He shrugged a shoulder, as if that should have been obvious to me.

"And you gave that up?"

"Yes," he said simply. His eyes were still locked on mine.

"Why?"

"Do you really need to ask?"

"Yes, I do."

A deep breath fortified him for his next confession. "The expression on your face that night... It killed me. I was sick— literally. I could not bear to touch her again."

I nodded, weighing my next question. "Do you miss her?"

"When would I have time to miss her? Every second I'm not with you, I'm thinking of you."

"Where have you been these last weeks, then?"

"I had a few... projects I needed to see through. Tonight was the last of them."

"Projects?"

That earned me a sigh. "As I said, I was one of the most powerful men in the city. It's a heady thing. Sometimes I engaged in a few ill-advised activities simply because I could."

"Such as..."

"There were a few boxing matches I had set about fixing before we wed. The rare card game that seemed to go in my favor. And a few endeavors with studding thoroughbreds. I am the owner of a particularly fine stallion that I occasionally stud. If, on some of those occasions, I provide the offerings of a similar-looking but much less-decorated stallion for the same price, who is to know? And if I choose to bet against those offspring in the future, who could say? Certainly no one who has any secrets they wish to remain hidden." Unlike before, he was not embarrassed. He took pride in these efforts. His old, over-confident self was seeping out. His voice was clear and lilting—unashamed.

"You mean to tell me that you are cheating gentlemen *and* bookmakers out of thousands of pounds."

"Was. The last match was tonight. And I have an agreement of sorts with a bookmaker or two."

"And you think secrets from your former mistress will save you from their wrath?"

"Well, it has worked thus far. But, as I said, that is done now."

It was my turn to draw a weary hand down my face. "So is that the lot of it? The fixed matches, cheating at cards, false studding, partial ownership of a brothel, a madame for a mistress, patronage at a brothel so frequently that you become a favorite, and possibly—but not probably—illegitimate children."

"I believe so. It's possible I've forgotten something."

"It's possible you've forgotten something... Of course it is."

"Celine..."

"You'll have to give me a moment, Gabriel. It's quite a list to take in."

"It's over now. I told you that."

"Yes, because your source of blackmail ended your arrangement."

He shot up, fists clenched at his sides. The settee rocked back onto two legs before righting itself with a *thunk*. "Because of you! I could not bear it if something happened to you. I could not bear to touch another woman. I could not withstand another night away from you." His tone had gone sharp, steely with frustration. He was back to wanting to strangle me again.

"Was no one else available at the brothel?"

In a single step he had both hands around my upper arms, dragging me to my feet. His hands seared me in place.

"Damn it all, Celine! I love you, you daft thing! Months I tried to stay away from you, and I could not do it. I tried to run you off and I came crawling back. I had the sole attention of the most famous courtesan in the whole of London and never, not once, did her most erotic touches affect me the way the brush of your hand against mine does. I've given up every independent source of income I have. Which, by the way, was quite a substantial income. But I've done it all without a thought merely because I knew you would not approve. I was the most powerful man in all of England, and you brought me to my knees with a look."

Oh...Oh my.

I stared, open-mouthed and wide-eyed. My body refused to obey my commands. He...

"You love me?" The words escaped unbidden, hanging hoarse in the air between us.

"Yes." The single syllable was low and thick with feeling. Underneath the dark irritation in his eyes, a passion burned. It was ablaze, incandescent, and unfathomably beautiful.

"I... me too. I love you too. I tried to listen, to stay away, but..." The rest of my declaration was delivered against his lips as they captured my own.

His hand cradled my jaw lovingly, but the rest of his kiss was all want. Lips and tongue slotted together in the most perfect of waltzes.

There were no more words of love that night; there was no need for them.

Fifteen

FOR ALL MY years in England, I had traveled little outside of London. It was an easy choice to abandon the season a few weeks early, traveling to Gabriel's ancestral home in Yorkshire.

The house was situated at the crest of a small hill. It featured a reddish-grey facade. Large bay windows covered the front of the home. The entry was well-maintained with a small pond in the center of a circular drive. To each side was a garden of wildflowers just past their peak, tips turning slightly brown in anticipation of winter. It was a lovely home, and I would be proud to serve as its mistress one day.

In the days and weeks after our disagreement, Gabriel had made an effort to be more attentive, which culminated in his slightly overeager expression as he searched my face for a reaction to his home. Whatever he found seemed to please him, and he made sure to point out various landmarks—far too distant for the eye to see.

He handed me from the carriage for my first unobstructed view. The butler, Reeves, and the housekeeper, Mrs. Talbot, managed a staff of more than twenty between them, all lined along the front entry of the house. It was then that I finally comprehended the enormity of my new station.

The management of the estate and several others fell to Her Grace for now, but one day I would be required to manage all of this. These people, and many others like them, would be dependent on me for their livelihood.

My voice was ropy as I greeted them as pleasantly as I could manage given my rising distress.

Though Mama taught me what she was able, my education on this subject was primarily theoretical. It was supplemented with a patchwork of observations from the homes where we overstayed our goodwill. Mama had not run her own home since we fled France.

I had never been more ill-prepared.

Gabriel eagerly pulled me by the wrist into the great house. Once inside, he released me when I gave a gentle tug. I spun slowly, taking in the place. Far from the blacks, whites, and grays of Hasket House in town, the interior was dressed in warm creams, eggshells, and butter yellows. The fabrics were soft velvets and well-spun damask silks.

"Mother is not particularly fond of Yorkshire weather," Gabriel explained, answering my unasked question with laughter barely contained in his tone.

With a light slap to his shoulder, I retorted, "I have never once said anything about the decor of Hasket House."

"You didn't have to say a word. Your relieved countenance said more than words ever could."

"Your mother knows what she likes and is very exacting."

"*Exacting* is one word for it. I have not been here in years. Four perhaps?"

"I imagine Yorkshire lacks some of the diversions that single gentlemen enjoy." I turned to him, teasing smile in place.

Mentions of Victoria and her profession had become a

sore spot for us both. Occasionally, I could not resist pressing that bruise, just to see if it had healed. The pain was lessening slightly, but my memory was too good for me to forget that night in the theater.

Instead of taking the bait, he replied, "You are absolutely correct. Until very recently, there was a distressing lack of a beautiful Marchioness."

"Marquise."

"Cee, you married an Englishman."

He pulled me back into him, wrapping an arm low about my waist while his other hand found his favored spot on my jaw. His grin was in full-blindingly beautiful force.

"*Mon amor*, you married a French woman. *Marquess* is a ridiculous word. I refuse to use it in relation to you. You are a Marquis and by extension I am a Marquise." The answering chuckle warmed me far more than the low-burning embers of the nearby hearth.

"And when I become a duke?"

"I shall be a duchess." He dropped a kiss on my jaw as a reward, his breath brushing across my collarbone purposefully.

"Not a *duchesse*?"

"No, I prefer duchess," I said primly.

"And you can pick and choose which you prefer?"

He was particularly handsome with his sardonic brow raised as he pulled away from the line he was kissing down my neck to smirk at me.

"*Oui*."

"I suppose I cannot fault your logic. Come, there is much more to show you. Such as the bedroom. Or do you prefer boudoir?"

"Oh boudoir, most definitely..."

~

His fingers trailed up and down my arm while I half dozed, swirling the letters of my name across his chest with my own fingers. The comforting thump of his heart gradually slowed under my cheek.

"What are you drawing?" His voice rumbled beneath my ear, more graveled due to our recent exertions.

"Just laying claim."

My head bounced slightly with his chuckle.

"I am yours. There's no need to write your name all over me."

I could only muster the effort to respond with a pleased hum. It was the work of another moment to gather my strength enough to lift my head and press a kiss to his heart.

"I had such good intentions in the carriage," he mused. "I was going to show you the house and the grounds. I was going to wait until after supper to ravish you."

"We have the rest of our lives for me to learn the lay of the land."

"We have the rest of our lives for this as well..."

His hand slid from my shoulder along the curve of my back, my waist, settling on my bottom with a possessive curve.

"But this is so much more enjoyable..." I retorted, stretching languorously.

"That it is... Still, I had a present for you."

At the mention of a gift, my strength was restored. I pressed myself up, using his chest for leverage and earning an undignified *oomf* for my efforts.

"Present?"

"I had quite forgotten how much you abhor gifts. I apologize, *ma cherie*." In spite of his efforts to keep a solemn countenance, the corner of his eyes crinkled with a hidden smile.

"You are a tease. And your accent really is atrocious, *mari*."

"Be nice, wife. Or I will not give you your gift."

"I am always nice," I protested.

"You are rarely nice. It is one of the reasons I love you."

He pressed a quick kiss to my forehead before rising from beneath the bedclothes. The motion left me to flop indelicately to my back and survey his form from the bed. He tragically located his breeches and began to don them.

"I can be nice... When it suits me. What have you gotten me?"

Gabriel dipped down to a nearby weathered, wooden trunk. He opened it with a resounding *thunk* while I admired his backside.

My question was deemed unnecessary; his only response was the rustling whisper of paper and the scraping of heavier objects from within the trunk. Then he pulled out a long, thin object, wrapped in a heavy, cream-colored cloth.

Something like a squeak escaped me and I clambered to my knees up, heedless of my present state of undress. That earned me a groan from my husband as he settled at the end of the bed, a poorly concealed object placed beside him.

"Celine, if you want your gift, you'll need to be less distracting."

I pulled the bedcovers up to my chest, tucking them underneath my arms while I shifted closer to him. Sufficiently hidden, I reached a hand toward what I suspected was finely honed steel.

Slowly, he pulled back first one side, then the other to reveal two small silver swords and a jeweled dagger, shining in the waning light cast through the window.

"You need a foil and a small sword. If you're going to learn, you may as well learn it all. I sent your measurements to the smith here. I prefer his work to the ones found in town. There's probably no real difference, of course. But he made my first sword as well."

I started with the dagger—less intimidating. The handle—

hilt?—was decorated in delicate vines and wildflowers, interlaced with gems of purple, red, and blue.

Carefully, I ran my thumb down the edge. This was no blunted blade. If I pressed with any force it would cut flesh.

The foil was next to be examined. It had no sharp edges, and the tip ended in a small button of steel. The small sword, like the dagger, was sharpened for blood.

Both swords were slightly shorter than ones I had seen gentlemen carry. The grip was smaller too. These were made for me.

"Once you've had some practice, we might move you to something full-length. Quite frankly, I don't wish to lose a limb while you're learning. And shorter means it's easier for me to dodge."

Finally, I glanced up from the glinting metal between us. His head was tilted, eyes examining, trying to glean a reaction from me.

I could not restrain my grin. "They are stunning. So beautiful that I will ignore the slight against my untested skills."

"You like them? Truly?"

"Of course! No one has ever given me a weapon before. I find I quite prefer them to the usual red roses and carnations."

"What about irises?" he asked with significance in his tone.

I gasped. "I knew it! I knew they were from you!"

"Guilty…" A pleased smirk slid over his face.

"They received a place of honor by my bedside." Distracted once more by a flash of silver, I added, "I do not suppose we can have a lesson now?"

"Why do you think I put on breeches? I suppose we should have a pair made for you as well. It will be difficult to practice in a gown. What are your thoughts on practicing outside in your shift?"

"My shift?"

"I think it the best option. Also, the most fetching," he said, his grin turning lecherous.

"Perhaps something a bit more covering. I've only been in residence for a few hours. I should at least wait until morning to scandalize the staff."

"If you must. Though I suspect the sounds you made an hour ago more than scandalized them all ready."

He yanked the bed linens from my form, ignoring my embarrassed, "Gabriel!"

"Best get up now, before I change my mind and trap you in this bed until next week."

"No, no. I want my lesson!" I protested through my own giggles as he pulled his shirt over his head before striding purposefully from the room.

Sixteen

SPRING FOUGHT to overtake the last dying breaths of winter. My own breath swirled in the crisp, late-morning air. In spite of the chill, I felt warm from my exercise, as I lunged and parried against my imagined foe.

Fencing had proved to be an activity I both enjoyed and excelled in. Perhaps more so even than Gabriel. It was not entirely clear to me whether the frequency of my wins against him were a kindness meant to encourage, a distraction at the sight of me in breeches, or the effects of my genuine talent. The thought of any three of the possibilities was enough to heat my chest further and birth a smile.

Several months in the country had shown Gabriel true to his word. Mysterious daylong and late-night meetings had ceased. He had become more forthright and open about his past, even sharing the occasional outdated bit of gossip with me.

This week he had to travel to town to meet with the solicitor. It was the longest we had been separated since our wedding, and his absence left me with a sense of anxiousness and purposelessness. Fencing, however, was an acceptable distraction in my time of need.

Gabriel and I had found our own little clearing off the massive gardens to practice. It was far enough from the house that neither of us felt concerned about my state of undress.

Green buds popped up from the surrounding bushes and trees. I was eager to see the estate in its full glory at last. Gabriel's great aunt had apparently been fond of the natural beauty of the midlands and had focused her energies on cultivating the wildflowers in pleasing ways.

Rose Hall was a natural beauty.

I parried in sixte with the same ease I found in the ballroom. The steps coming as naturally to me as those of a quadrille.

A sharp *snap* came from somewhere behind me and I froze, my blood following suit. I waited, breath caught, for the familiar warmth of my husband's eyes on my person, for the kind tones of Jane or Reeves.

Nothing.

My hand tightened on my foil instinctively. I was left wishing like hell that my small sword was not lying several feet away on the bench, useless. Breath tight, I turned.

A girl, or woman, I suppose—it was difficult to discern— stood before me. She was tall, but thin. Skeletal, even. Her head was overlarge on her frame and cocked to the side, studying me with interest. She wore a gossamer white nightdress in spite of the chill and late-morning hour. Her skin was as pale as the crisp muslin of the gown. There was no color on her gaunt, sharp cheeks, save the shadows where they sank into her skull. Her lips, too, were thin and near the same translucent shade.

The wind brushed through her hair, which hung loose in an inky black curtain. It, alone appeared healthy—glossy—as though it held all the life she still possessed. She swayed slightly in the breeze, a sapling bending to its will.

It was her eyes that I could not escape from. Clear and blue as a crystal lake framed by dark lashes. Her stare was intent, unblinking, enthralling. At the same time, I thought perhaps she was not seeing me at all. Skilled though I was at reading people, her thoughts were impregnable. It was entirely disconcerting.

Through it all she said nothing. One by one my fingers loosened on the grip of my foil, and I rose from the instinctive guard I had found.

Strange she may be, but physically... She seemed as though one gust of wind would blow her away.

I ignored the uneasy prickling down my spine—so different from the feel of Gabriel's eyes. Discomfiture in the face of such illness was no excuse for poor manners.

"Are you unwell?" I asked. "You should sit. Please."

I gestured toward the bench where my small sword lay, my eyes never leaving her own.

I was half afraid she would collapse right there. She certainly weighed little, but it was still more than I could reasonably carry all the way to the house.

"I wanted to greet the sunshine girl," she said, as though that was a perfectly sensible explanation. Her voice was small, high, and artificially childlike. It was as if she had bumped it up an octave. The cadence had an odd lyrical quality. It was disconcerting enough for me to finally shutter the prolonged eye contact. My gaze flicked away to the sky.

A brief glance was enough to confirm that the murky gray morning haze would not abate anytime soon. Certainly, there was no sun to be found.

"I really think you should sit," I reiterated as I stepped toward her, trying gently to direct her toward the bench. I couldn't bring myself to touch her, though. Instead, my hand hovered an inch or so off her back.

She took one single step before groaning pitifully.

With all the care I possessed, I forced myself to press my hand to her back and guide her to the bench.

Her skin was too thin and too soft through her gown. The divots of her spine were too sharp and too mountainous underneath her flesh.

Finally she acquiesced under my palm, but her steps were weak and her muscles quivered under the effort. The small sword was easily removed from the bench while I gestured for her to take its place.

Seated at last, she raised both hands to hover just off her temples. A headache, perhaps?

I perched on the edge of the bench next to her, unsure how to assist.

Her hands, still an inch or so off her temples, were all bone. The skin hung loose with reddish-gray patches on her palms. Those hands were probably lovely once. The fingers were long and elegant and even in her weakened state her nails were well-maintained.

All of her was, really.

She was clearly very ill, but her gown was starched and pressed, her hair brushed and tied back with a fine ribbon, and her impossibly pale skin was clean.

Someone cared for her—would be missing her.

But how to help her? I had no idea where she came from. It took several minutes to get her to the bench. How was I to get her to the house? I could not possibly leave her here. Could I?

I settled on an easier question first.

"Can you tell me your name?"

Her hands fell to her lap and her eyes snapped back to

mine. There was a clarity, an understanding there that had been absent before.

And then she answered. "*Pour cinq francs tu peux m'appeler come tu veux.*" Her accent was bawdy. The tone had shifted as well, the childlike musicality vanished. In its place was a serrated bite.

She stared directly *through* me now. Her chin dipped low and her eyes held mine from below her brow. The clear, blue lake was frozen now, iced over.

My spine froze as well. My hand clenched desperately, wishing for the hilt that lay feet away on the ground.

"*Mademoiselle...*" I drew the word out as long as possible, waiting for inspiration that never came.

She shifted in her seat, her expression clearing and her posture relaxing. "I've frightened the sunshine girl, oh dear." The sing-song quality had returned with her shift back to English. It was as though nothing had happened, as if she hadn't broken into crass French a mere moment ago.

She began to sway to and fro on the bench, dancing to music only she could hear.

"He's coming. He's afraid that *he* found me. It doesn't matter, though. In the end they'll all belong to the girl. None for me."

I was... not going to address that. I would have to leave her here to get help. There was no way she would make the walk to the house. And if I was being quite honest, I had no desire for her bewildering company.

"If you'll just stay here, *mademoiselle*, I will return with help." I held my hands up in some bizarre attempt to placate her lest she lash out again.

"There is no need. Help is here," she replied calmly, no lilting tone or eerie French. That change was nearly as distressing as the others.

I fought it down. "*Mademoiselle*, I cannot help you—"

"Adriane!" A sharp baritone rang out.

The masculine voice came from some distance away, but it was in the direction of the hedge row that the girl—Adriane? —had appeared at.

I had no way of knowing if this man was any safer—or saner—than the wraith before me, but at least his voice lacked the childlike ringing that set me on edge.

"Here!" I called out, rising to find the man. I could only hope desperately that this was, in fact, Adriane before me.

The man burst through the hedges, panting harshly. Clad in breeches with a sword sheathed at his side, a shirt with half-done cravat, and no waistcoat or greatcoat to be seen, he looked precisely as disheveled as he sounded.

He stood only a few inches taller than me with a tight build wrapped in finely honed muscles. His ash-brown hair was close-cropped. The man was young, certainly not more than thirty, but his face was all harsh angles, giving him a worldly countenance. A square jaw met with cheekbones sharp enough to cut diamonds. They were hollowed, like hers, but his were entirely natural, fitting. There was no hint of starvation or illness in him. And his eyes were the deep navy of sapphires.

And they were only for her.

"Adriane! You should not be out, sweetling."

Her only reply was a pained, trilled moan as her hands returned to her temples.

The man dropped to his knees before her. Catching her hands in his own and squeezing, he pressed a gentle kiss to each palm and then her pained temple.

I may as well have been a statue for all the attention he paid me, but I still felt the part of intruder.

"How did you get so far?" he asked. "You must be chilled."

"I wanted to greet the sunshine."

His head fell back a few inches, hinging on his neck. But

he gave no other outward indication that this speech was as nonsensical as it seemed.

"Of course. But you know I worry. Perhaps we can meet the sun on the veranda tomorrow?" He was sincere, kind in tone. Devotion was plain on his face and in his manner as he gently tucked a loose curl behind her ear, resting a hand on her jaw. Cherishing.

"The sun won't come out tomorrow."

"Your sun would not dare hide. Not if you wished to see it. I won't allow it." He added a firm nod to that declaration, ridiculous as it was.

I could watch in silence no longer. This was not a moment for me. "Pardon me..."

Finally, he turned to me. There was no surprise in his gaze. Instead, I saw only pain. It receded from my prying eyes, leaving nothing but exhaustion in its wake. He rose back to his feet with a weary sigh.

"You're a new one," he stated, disinterest in his tone and attitude.

"I beg your pardon?"

He made no effort to conceal his answering eye roll. "Oh, good Lord. Does Her Grace pay you extra to fake the accent?"

"Excuse me?"

"*C'est probablement le pire accent que j'aie jamais entendu.*" His French was impeccable. And the content infuriating.

"*Peut-être n'avez-vous jamais parlé à une française,*" I retorted.

He switched back to English with a sneer. "I've spoken to plenty of Frenchwomen. In France. Where I fought. Perhaps you should speak to one. Your French is worse than your accent. And the breeches? Are those something some ridiculous fashion plate told Her Grace was in style?"

"I am not a servant! I am Lady Celine Hasket, Marquise of

Rycliffe and you will speak to me with the respect I am due," I snapped.

The weariness evaporated from him. His spine straightened and his eyes shot to his lady, inspecting her from toes to crown. Seemingly satisfied that she was in no worse health than she had been when she'd wandered off, he spun sharply back to face me. His hand fell to the hilt of his sword.

Instinctively, my hand clenched around air as my stomach dropped. A brief glance to the side told me what I already knew. My own swords lay feet away under the bench.

"Where is he?" the man bit out in a harsh growl as his eyes scanned the landscape ceaselessly.

"Who?"

"Hasket! Where is he?"

"Gabriel..." Adriane's vibrato whine of my husband's name drifted across the wind.

My body understood before my mind, ice spreading through my veins.

"London," I choked out. It was a poor choice, letting the man know my husband was so far away, but his posture was entirely defensive. He had not drawn the sword.

Rather than advancing toward me, he backed up to Adriane, his right hand hovering in front of her, palm wide, keeping her in place.

He was left-handed. An entirely inane thought, but it was better than the one pressing against my memory, desperate for release.

He gave another scan of the area before straightening and dropping his hand from his sword.

"How long?" he growled.

"A few more days, perhaps a week."

His gaze darted back and forth. It was clear he did not believe my words.

Finally, he turned to face me head-on, steel, indigo eyes boring into mine. "You never saw us. Do you understand?"

I could only nod dully. He stared for a beat longer, before turning back to her—Adriane.

Impossibly gently, he urged her to stand. He shushed her answering distressed wordless whine.

"Can I carry you, sweetling?"

Her reply was unintelligible to my ears, but he took it as permission. He lifted her into his arms with ease before sweeping out of the clearing. His stride was unburdened by the added weight of the woman's sickly frame. His eyes never paused in their ceaseless darting.

Their absence was palpable, the wind whispering just a touch louder to compensate for the new silence.

I was left to gather my swords from beneath the bench and make my way back to the house. All the while, my husband's early warning tickled the back of my mind.

"I don't seduce innocents. Not any longer."

Seventeen

THREE DAYS.

Gabriel did not return for three days.

Three days of haunting, lyrical utterances tracing along my spine. Three nights of dreams filled with panicked, darting sapphire eyes. Seventy-two hours of my husband's warning playing in a ceaseless loop through my mind.

"I don't seduce innocents. Not any longer."

"The consequences are too great."

"I am not a good man."

He'd been referring to her. I had never been more certain of anything.

Shortly before supper on the third evening, he returned, putting an end to the irritated pacing of my chambers. He brushed a quick kiss to my unresponsive mouth before rushing past me to clean and dress.

We had enjoyed an informal table in the country. I typically chose to sit beside him rather than across the great expanse of table. I lamented that choice now. Now that the blindfold had been ripped off.

Now that I understood.

I sat at the table, unhearing as he prattled on excitedly about Lord only knew what. He paused only for bites of tasteless meat and dry potatoes. At least, that was my experience of them as I took performative mouthfuls.

The question bubbled inside me—over and over in a ceaseless, unending, infinite circle through my mind to the exclusion of all else.

It was little surprise when it burst forth unbidden.

"Who is Adriane?"

The fork slipped from his hand and landed with a cacophonous *clank* on his plate. He froze, midchew, and stared wide-eyed at me before swallowing his bite thickly, his throat bobbing with the effort.

"Where did you hear that name?"

Something about the tentative tone and evasive nature of the question sparked my ire. "Answer the question, Gabriel."

"I will. I was just..."

"Evading. Don't you dare lie to me."

He raised a placating hand in front of him, palm forward. "I have never lied to you."

"No, you just neglected to give me the entire truth."

"That is unfair. I told you. I told you on our second meeting that I had seduced an innocent."

"Not like that you didn't, and you know it."

He pinched the bridge of his nose between his forefinger and thumb. At least he managed to look suitably ashamed. For what he'd done to that woman.

"I've done many terrible, amoral things. You know that... But Adriane... It was unforgivable."

"Tell me," I demanded.

"Cee..."

"Did you force her?"

"What? Of course not."

He had the audacity to look offended at that question. As if *that* was a step too far. Lying, cheating, gambling, fraud, seduction, and abandonment were fine—of course. But force would be beyond him.

The worst part was that I desperately wanted to believe him incapable of it too.

"Then it cannot possibly be worse than my imaginings. Tell me."

With a weary sigh he began his confession. "I spent more time here, at Rose Hall, when I was young. When my grandmother was still alive, Mother would send us here for much of the season."

I nodded, waiting for him to continue his—thus far—uninteresting story. Such a banal starting point would not distract me from my ire.

"Xander is so much younger than I am. We did not play together often. But the steward's son, William, was only a year or two my junior. We did not have much in common—he was more interested in his studies—but he was my best option."

"Go on," I insisted.

I earned another sigh. I was beginning to loathe that sound. At last, he continued.

"Father was so fond of him. He even funded William's education... Sent him to Eton with me. Will was so damned studious. Father was always comparing us. And every time, I was found wanting. I had no interest in investing the kind of effort required to be as good a student as William. There was no fun to be had in that."

I hadn't known Gabriel as a boy. But I could well believe it of him. Though he was far from lazy, given the choice, he would find the path of least resistance. In fact, I would be far from surprised to learn I was the first thing he had ever attempted to resist.

I twirled an impatient finger in the air, bidding him continue.

"I began to use the opposite approach. Studied as little as possible... Started boxing and gaming... Spent my evenings in brothels instead of the library, that sort of thing... I was quite content with that sort of life."

"I am all astonishment. Truly," I sniped.

His only response was to drag a hand across his face.

"Then the LaMorte's let Crawford Park. It's about three miles east. Grandmother had the family over to supper, as was proper. And there, Will saw Adriane for the first time... The entire meal, he stared at her, wide-eyed and open-mouthed. It was as if she'd hung all the stars in the sky. Besotted at first sight... He even wrote her poetry. It was entirely pathetic." He broke off with a bitter sort of chuckle.

Certainly, if the man I met was William, he wore his love etched in the lines of his face. I could well believe he was capable of poetry. But pathetic... There was nothing pathetic about the way that man—*William*—loved Adriane.

"But Adriane... She only had eyes for me. The harder Will tried, the more she looked to me. It was a game to her..."

Gabriel's eyes had found the table and fixed themselves there.

He continued his speech directly to the walnut wood. "Somehow he decided that if he had more impressive career prospects she would finally look at him... Her father is untitled but landed. Nothing could have induced LaMorte to allow his daughter to wed the son of a steward. But William couldn't be convinced of that. So my father agreed to facilitate his entry into Oxford. Will thought to become a solicitor... Father was so damn proud." He shook off the memory, thumb brushing over a nick in the table I'd never noticed before.

I didn't know His Grace well, but I could find no lie in Gabriel's tale. Nothing in his explanation rang false. And his broken tone... the hollow note in his voice... Sympathy welled in my chest, unbidden and unwanted.

"I was still young... hadn't yet learned how to gamble properly. I lost a fair amount of money, which sent my father into quite the rage. He said—shouted, really—a great many things. The most painful of which was when he told me he wished William was his son instead of me.

"I think it hurt so very much because I knew it was true, always had been. In that moment he snatched away any comfort I could find in plausible deniability. Right after that was when Adriane found me."

His smile was wry, but still aimed at the table. The nick held his interest as he dug a well-manicured thumbnail into it. It was an unconscious, unseen destruction.

"There was someone who wanted *me*, not William. I had no intention of wedding her. To be honest, the way she would stare at me was unnerving... She was quite strange as well, always talking in some riddle that no one but her understood. But I was feeling sorry for myself. And she made me feel like a man. She pulled me into the horse barn, of all places. I took her in a barn." He broke off with another bitter chuckle.

"After we finished, she asked when I would speak to her father. I just laughed. I returned to town the next morning."

For the first time since he began, Gabriel met my gaze. His eyes searched mine, desperately seeking absolution.

"Will appeared at Rycliffe Place one morning about three months later. He was raving about how I'd ruined her and that her family threw her out. I don't even know how her family learned of it. I didn't know they would actually toss her out." His voice broke on the last word.

Gabriel's hand found mine, pulling it to his chest. To his heart. "I haven't touched another innocent, not until our wedding night. I swear it." There was an unfamiliar desperation in his gaze. He was willing me to believe him.

Silence hung between us, its invisible presence tangible, palpable in the air. Or perhaps that was her—Adriane.

Finally, I could bear it no longer. "Is that the last of it? The last secret?"

"Yes."

"I mean it, Gabriel. No more half-truths. No more evasions. No more distractions. This has to be all of it."

"It is. There's nothing else."

I nodded to myself, then yanked my hand free from his chest.

"I need some time. I need to think."

"Cee..."

"No, Gabriel. You owe me this."

His lower lip was caught between his teeth, trapping his protests by force. With a calming breath, he replied, "all right. If that is what you need."

"Thank you."

THE HALL CLOCK CHIMED MIDNIGHT. One. Two. How had I never noticed the volume before? The ticking, too, echoed through the solid frame of my door.

The bed linens were stiff with disuse and smelled of laundry powder instead of bergamot.

My feet were frozen to blocks of ice, but the rest of me was too hot.

I had chosen to retire to my own chambers tonight for the first time in my marriage. And my chambers were horrid. Oh, I supposed, in an objective sense they were perfectly well-situated. But tonight, with my husband just through the door... And after more than a week apart...

But my husband was the same man who had seduced a

young lady and turned her into that... that wraith. What had the world done to her after Gabriel discarded her?

Flipping my pillow for the thousandth time to the cooler side, I was met with disappointment. It was too hot, just like the other side.

It was ridiculous. Discomfort and a lack of sleep was hardly going to help me think. Surely I could just...

With a sigh I abandoned all of my principles. I got out of bed and padded over to the adjoining door and pressed it open with quiet caution. I needn't have made that effort.

"Celine?" he called. There was no sleep in my husband's voice. None of the familiar, rough half growl he favored me with in the early morning hours.

My eyes adjusted to the dimmer lighting. The fire had burned lower than my own, and the screen was thicker than the one designated for me. Gabriel was sprawled on his back on the half of the bed that I usually claimed. One arm was wrapped around a pillow—mine. It was the same way he usually curled around my shoulders.

What principles? I had none.

"May I sleep in here?" I asked, hating the hopefulness in my tone.

"Please."

He rolled to his side with a boyish, charming eagerness. Had I *ever* possessed principles? Surely not, if the ease with which I removed my pillow and curled against his arm was any indication. Gabriel's response was slower, tentative, but his hand came to rest in its home, low in the divot between my ribcage and hip.

"This does not mean I forgive you," I murmured into the dark.

"Right."

"It just means I cannot sleep."

"All right."

The hand tightened on my waist—just a little—and he swallowed thickly. His breath evened out, deepening into the steady rhythm that usually lulled me to my dreams. The tension in his muscles assured me he was no closer to sleep than I was.

"Did you look for her?"

He was silent for a beat too long. I thought perhaps I had been mistaken, that he was asleep. But then he answered.

"No. I hadn't heard she had been banished from her home until some months later. Not until Will came asking after her. He threw a punch when I made a bawdy joke. He was such a skinny little thing and two years my junior. But he was determined... Over and over, he kept scrambling back up, following me. He could barely stand by the end. I had to knock him out to get him to leave me be. Afterward, I wrote to my mother, and she confirmed the girl was gone but did not know the reason."

"Would you have married her? If you had known?"

Gabriel hesitated for a moment before replying, "I promised not to lie to you."

"No, then?"

"I would love to tell you that I would have wed her. But I truly do not know. I like to think I would not have taken her in the first place. But it was probably inevitable. If it hadn't happened then, it would have happened some other time. She was determined. And I hated William. There was nothing else in the world that would have hurt him that way. The idea, using her against him, was always there. I think she wanted to hurt him too. She liked his attentions, the way he would try even harder when she made eyes at me. She certainly never discouraged him, at any rate. And she was even more flirtatious with me in his presence."

"What happened to William?" I asked, though I was almost positive I knew that answer.

"He enlisted. It was three, perhaps four years ago. I have not heard since. His father died, and my father hasn't mentioned him since his enlistment. He was disappointed, wanted better for his protege than that. I assume Will went to France."

He had. I was certain of it.

And there he had found Adriane.

No gently bred young lady spoke French in such a lewd tone. And no steward's son spoke French with such fluency. Not without practical experience. There was something heartachingly beautiful in that. A man facing war and death to find his love... Searching boarding houses and brothels to find her. Only to find a senseless apparition in her place.

"It's ironic, I suppose." Gabriel's bitter tone cut through my musings. "In the end he finally fell from Father's grace. He probably died for his troubles."

I could hear the thick guilt in his voice, raw instead of honeyed. I considered remaining silent. And I remembered the look of naked adoration in William's eyes as he knelt before Adriane. It was not my secret to tell. But.... Was withholding this not the same thing he had done to me?

"Promise me something?"

"Anything."

I pressed myself up and turned to meet his gaze. Gabriel followed, rising, keeping us close. Even in the dim light I could read the open, desperate sincerity. "If I tell you something, you will take no action."

"What?"

"You will do nothing with the information I give you."

"What would I—"

"Swear to me," I pressed again.

"I swear. Anything you want."

"He's alive."

"What?"

"William is alive. I think. I did not actually get his name, but I'm almost certain it was him," I explained.

"How?"

"I met Adriane. He came to collect her."

"You met Adriane?"

"Yes."

"And William?"

"I believe so. Once he learned my identity, he was more concerned about where you were than introducing himself."

He wore a flabbergasted expression poorly. His eyes flitted back and forth as he parsed memories for some way to make sense of my intelligence.

"Where? How?"

"She came wandering over while I was practicing my footwork. As I said, he came to collect her. He asked me not to tell. I should not have. But I have just accused you of withholding information... It seemed hypocritical."

"So he found her then." He flopped back onto the bed. The tension melted from his arms.

"More or less," I replied.

"I beg your pardon?"

"She is not well."

"How do you know?"

"Aside from babbling a lot of nonsense about sunshine? She was skeletal. And her head clearly pained her. He was worried she would catch a chill when he found her. There were grey patches, like a rash. Or something like one." He swallowed thickly at that.

"Pox..."

"Possibly. Probably."

"You are all right? No one hurt you?"

"No. She made me uneasy but did not try to touch me. He was ready to run you through when he thought you might be nearby. But he never made a move toward me." He relaxed slightly at that intelligence.

"So when you asked me who she was?"

"I suspected, but I did not know for certain."

"And if I had lied…"

"If you had lied, we would be having a very different conversation," I said, warning in my tone.

He rose again, onto his side, and tucked me into his chest. "Celine, I do not have the words…"

A sigh broke from my chest. I was so, so unbearably tired. And sleep was a million miles away. At the end of this conversation, if I was lucky.

"I will move past this. I'm certain of it. I just…. She was so… When you first told me you had seduced an innocent, I assumed a lady had her marital prospects damaged. Perhaps wed someone a little older or a little poorer than she had intended. I did not consider that she had been thrown out to make her way to a Parisian brothel. That her family would leave her to descend into sickness and madness. It was difficult to see. To realize the man I love, the man responsible for all my happiness, was also responsible for so much heartache. It is taking some time to adjust my perspective."

"Cee, I would never. Not to you," he protested.

"But I am no different from her. Not really. I happened to meet you when you were in a better frame of mind. Perhaps I am luckier in my family than she was. But the differences… It comes down to timing and luck. Our evening on the terrace could have just as easily ended in my ruin."

"Celine, never. I was half in love with you before we exchanged a single word. And if I had failed you, if I hadn't done the gentlemanly thing, Champaign was right there to take my place. The rest were in line behind him."

"I suppose we'll never know. I just need some time,

Gabriel. And some rest. I have not slept well since you left. Will you hold me? Just hold me?"

"Forever if you'll have me."

"Tonight will do for present." I settled back into the crook of his arms. Comfortable once again. Except for the feet. I wriggled them between his legs for warmth. He gave his requisite yelp before tightening his arms around me.

"Go to sleep," he whispered, brushing a kiss to my crown.

Eighteen

RYCLIFFE PLACE, LONDON - MAY 13, 1809

"Please...."

"No." My husband's reply was little more than a discontented groan from underneath the bedcovers. After two years of marriage, I knew that tired moan well. I knew his other sounds as well.

"Please, *mon amor*?"

"No."

"I suppose, if you will not join me, my breeches and I shall have to practice all by ourselves..." That earned a slight shifting of the blankets, and a disheveled head and singular, bleary mahogany eye popped into view. The eye made a slow perusal down my form.

"Celine... Come back to bed." A muscular forearm shuffled free from its fabric trappings and tried to grab my waist as I brushed past.

"Gabriel, I wish to practice."

"Celine, I wish to ravish you. Then practice. Perhaps a nap between."

"We attend the races today. If I return to bed, you will be useless until we must leave."

"You were not calling me useless last night. In fact, I remember you begging me to never stop." His hand finally succeeded at catching my waist and pulling me onto the bed with him. He was much more awake than he had been a few moments ago. "We will practice after the races..."

"Liar. Your mother's ball is this evening."

"Five minutes. I promise you will forget all about practice."

"Two."

"What?"

"You have two minutes to convince me. If I have not forgotten... Then practice."

"Challenge accepted," he whispered, smiling into a kiss.

"WE'LL BE LATE," Gabriel whispered, harsh and low, in my ear as I adjusted a curl in the mirror.

"If only you had concerned yourself with that this morning. If you continue to rush me, I will slow down."

"Cee, I have wagers to place."

"Oh, of course. Wagers. Please tell me these are aboveboard?" The chagrined tug of his brows in the mirror said more than words.

"I never lie to you."

"Very well, do not tell me. I like to make my bets with my own intuition." That earned me a crooked grin.

"You base them on which horse you think looks finest."

"Precisely. Intuition."

"And your intuition seems to prefer anything in the black variety."

I shrugged. "They are pretty. Father had a black stallion. I remember watching him ride."

"Sorry, darling. I did not realize." He tugged gently at the loose curl by my ear.

"Do not be sorry. Without the benefit of understanding or experience, it seems as good a selection criteria as any other."

"Quite right," he answered and pressed a kiss to my temple. His gaze caught on my necklace, and he adjusted the pendant to lie frontward with wandering fingers.

"I thought we were late."

"You are an unbearably beautiful distraction," he said with a groan. "I shall await you in the hall."

It was a beautiful day for the races. Gabriel was off placing our wagers.

I had indeed requested he place a wager on Storms Kiss, the only inky black stallion racing today. Gabriel had not stopped talking about Peppercorn Junction in the carriage. I felt confident his wager would yield a substantial return whereas mine would not.

Still, I could hardly bring myself to wager on a horse with such a ridiculous name.

I found myself pressed in the middle of Gabriel's family— my family in truth. In an effort to ease Her Grace's burden while she directed the preparations for tonight's ball, I requested the company of the younger Hasket siblings. Everyone involved in the discussion seized on my suggestion with enthusiasm.

Davina, determined to prove herself an adult at four and ten, had borrowed my jeweled hairband and my feathered evening fan. It was quite too much for a day at the races, but she was too excited to discourage.

She had set out with the intention to learn the subtle language of the fan. But now, she was chiefly occupied with tossing it in the air and catching it. Up and down it flipped and spun. She caught it and dropped it in equal measure while she bickered with Xander.

As usual, it was a struggle to maintain a disapproving facade to cover my laughter.

Across the crowd, I caught the delectable sight of the broad back that still bore marks from my nails from this morning. He was chatting with a smaller man, but I could see little over my husband's shoulders beyond an ash-brown head. Something about the scene, so routine—commonplace, really —was wrong. Perhaps the tension with which my husband held his frame? The clenching of the fist at his side?

I rose to offer my services as rescue when he turned his back on the gentleman and strode back toward us. By the time my gaze returned to the man, I could only catch his back. Shorter than Gabriel, athletic in build. A needling familiarity pricked as my gaze followed his retreat into the crowd.

I could not place him, could not recall a name.

Gabriel found his seat beside me and handed me a lemonade. He made a valiant effort to relax, but his muscles were coiled, an instant from action.

"Who was that?" I asked.

He did not turn to me, instead focused solely on the track. Still, after nearly two years of marriage, I knew my husband. He was trying to determine the most pleasant way to deliver an unpleasant truth.

"Later?" he asked.

With a sigh I took a sip. Not a lie, at least. "Promise?"

That drew his attention from the dirt track and beaten grass. "Yes."

Silently he brought a heavy palm to my knee, searing me through my gown, even after all this time. He offered a quiet squeeze of promise, before releasing me.

Just then, Davina managed to flip the fan directly at the

brim of Xander's top hat which landed in a nearby puddle. The commotion pulled my attention from my husband's recalcitrance.

My services as mediator were required, lest there be bloodshed.

With a sharp look at Dav, I snapped my hand out for the fan. Silently, she handed it over. Her acquiescence may have been wordless, but it was anything but pleasant. Arms crossed over her chest and mouth twisted into a petulant pout, she was not going to apologize of her own volition.

"I'm sorry, Xander. I should not have let her play like that," I said, directing my attention toward the fuming young gentleman in front of me.

"She did it on purpose," Xander protested. At twenty, he was a man grown, but I suspected something about Davina would always leave him sounding like a disgruntled boy.

I shot a glance toward the culprit, and she merely raised an overgrown brow in confirmation.

"I suspect she did. Which is why she will not have it again until she can act with decorum."

A glance at Gabriel confirmed he was still seated, eagerly awaiting Peppercorn's race, no doubt.

I bit back an eye roll before calling out to him. "Gabriel, dearest, would you take your brother to clean up while Davina and I have a chat?"

"But—"

"Gabriel... The horses aren't even out of the stables yet."

"all right, yes. Come with me, Xander." He stepped out of the stands and grabbed his brother's arm, rushing him along.

I directed Davina back to the stands with a shooing motion and trundled in after her.

"You can hardly blame me."

"Davina..."

"But it's so easy... And he never wants to have fun anymore."

My fingers found the bridge of my nose and pinched of their own volition. "Davina, I promise that someday you will understand. But Xander is under immense pressure. And your needling him does not make that any easier."

"If he were less stuffy, he would have friends."

"Xander needs to behave as a gentleman ought. Now that he's taken his place in society, his behavior reflects on all of us —and most especially you. You should be grateful he is taking it seriously. Especially since Gabriel saw no need."

"But—"

"I mean it, Dav. You need to stop tormenting him on purpose."

She made no further protests but turned back to the track with her arms crossed and her face fully set in the pout. I could only hope something I said made the slightest impact.

Turning my attention back toward the track with her, I caught sight of the wired form and sable-brown hair of the man from before. He was leaning against a railing across the way, directly in front of me. At first I saw only his profile. The proud, straight nose and angular jaw strangely familiar.

Then he turned, and impossibly blue eyes found mine instantly.

And I knew.

I had not thought of Adriane and William in months. Certainly not since we returned from the country last spring.

Now, though, I could not look away. He pinned me in place with his inscrutable expression and the clenched tick of his jaw.

Davina drew my attention with an indelicate tap on my shoulder. "How much longer before the races start?"

I fought an eye roll. "A few more minutes, I suspect."

When I looked back to the rail again, he was gone.

Gabriel returned moments later with a slightly less distraught Xander in tow.

A quick studying look was all he needed to read me. "Did he approach you?" He whispered from my side.

"No. I just saw him across the way. It startled me when I managed to place him."

"Are you well?"

I considered the question for a moment. There had been something haunted, aching in the set of William's posture and the depths of his gaze.

"She is gone, isn't she?"

"It seems likely."

"What did he want?"

"He wants to talk, later this week. Probably, he is hoping for funds for the funeral furnisher or something of that nature."

Placated for the moment and distracted by the start of the race, the track commanded our attention for the rest of the afternoon.

As expected, Gabriel won a substantial sum on a long shot. I lost a modest one on a dark horse. The rest of the *ton* lost a great deal on Flashdance. I chose to refrain from asking my husband questions about that happenstance. In spite of the brief moments of levity, it was an enjoyable afternoon.

There was little in the way of time to dwell on William or Adriane after returning to the house. I dressed for Her Grace's ball with care. A dusky mauve gown with heavier beading near the bodice that continued down to the hem in increasing sparseness.

Gabriel made every effort to recreate the morning's dalliance. When he was finally dressed, he wore more than one rouge kiss trailing down his torso under his waistcoat for his efforts. It was no matter, the shade did not flatter my gown anyhow.

A few minutes after we arrived at Hasket House, my husband disappeared with a few of the gentlemen. I hovered on the edge of the dance floor, certain he would return to me in time to claim the first set.

When, just as the first chords began, I felt the familiar warmth of Gabriel's gaze on the back of my neck, it was no surprise.

"Do you know how long it took me to work up the courage to speak to you that night?" His honeyed voice danced along my spine, his hand trailing inches behind. "You were standing right here, looking every bit as beautiful as you do tonight."

I turned with a smile that was all for him. "Is that why you forgot to request my consent for our dance?"

"No. I simply did not wish to give you the opportunity to decline." I could hear the crooked grin in his voice. His lips, however, only twitched with the effort to conceal it.

"You should ask me now."

"Dance with me, darling?"

"Always."

Nineteen

WE ABSOLUTELY SHOULDN'T HAVE BEEN DOING this in the carriage. It was improper. The driver and footman were almost certainly aware of our antics in spite of my teeth digging into my lower lip with ferocity.

The second the door had shut out the outside world, Gabriel's hands and lips had been on me. Everywhere. All at once. With the kind of desperation that left me stifling gasps and moans.

My lips broke free on a ragged gasp when his fingers twisted right *there* and his teeth nipped like *that*.

"Quiet, darling," he breathed against my neck where his tongue soothed the flesh he'd just marked. "Remember, all of your sounds are mine. The moans, the whimpers, the pants— they're only for me."

And I was trying to remember that. Truly I was. Not for his reasoning of course, even if his possessive tone did cause my stomach to flip in delight. But because we absolutely should not be doing this here. It was no less improper the way the heel of his hand worked against my mound in the most perfect rhythm.

Another sound must have escaped me because I could feel Gabriel's grin against my collarbone when he whispered, "If you can't keep quiet, I'll have to stop."

I didn't give my hand permission to grasp his wrist, clutching him desperately in place. But it did, scrambling to hold him steady, to increase the pressure from this infuriating teasing.

He tutted, his tone smug and full of false disappointment. "I suppose there are other ways to keep you quiet. What do you think, Celine? Should I gag you?"

Yes. I wanted to agree, desperately. We'd only done that a few times. Gabriel preferred to hear me. And I'd only done it once to him—I adored the way he spoke to me. But when I caught the glint in his eyes, I knew precisely which game he wanted to play. Our newest one.

"No, no. I'll be good. I promise," I whispered fervently, yanking his lips back to mine to seal my false promise with a kiss that was nearly as filthy as what his hand was doing under my skirts.

Another groan threatened to escape when he added a third finger, and I caught my lip between teeth again.

"Well done," he teased. Slipping the bodice of my gown down with his other hand, he freed a breast.

I managed the kiss, the drugging, sensual swirl of his tongue in hard-earned silence. But when his teeth dragged along my nipple, when he slipped his thumb over the bud at my center, and when he twisted his fingers at precisely the same moment... No dam in the world could have held back the keening whimper that escaped me.

"Oh Celine, you promised." His amusement was clear in his tone, too pleased with his ability to take me apart to feign disapproval. "I'm trying to do important work here, and you're interrupting."

The hand not currently working my quim found its way

to my mouth. He was careful, ensuring I could breathe freely, but his hand was so large it covered the lower half of my face. His fingers easily curled along the hinge of my jaw.

Satisfied with whatever he saw in my eyes—dazed lust, most likely—he dipped his head back to the other breast.

The thumb on my nub worked me in tight circles, his fingers twisting precisely the way he knew I adored. I was there, right at the edge. The precipice.

Oh, I was wanton. Utterly shameless for this man. I'd done precisely as he wished because I wished it too.

I wasn't surprised when it happened. After all, I knew this game too. When the pressure of his thumb against me vanished, leaving only the heel of his hand, my whimper was muffled under his other palm, and the stuttering movement of my hips was instinctive.

It wasn't enough. I knew it wouldn't be. He did too.

"Ah-ah... I think we both know you cannot remain quiet, even with my assistance. You'll have to wait until we're home."

The game had seemed such a good idea before, when the pressure was still right, when release had been something in the distance. Now I was panting harshly against his palm and aching inside, clenching on too-still fingers.

So close. So impossibly far away.

And then he did the unimaginable and slipped his hand out from under my skirt.

My pleas were unintelligible against his hand. Gabriel only chuckled, sliding damp fingers across oversensitive nipples before righting my bodice. Desperate and aching, I clutched at his hand, trying to bring it back to my center. Under the skirt, over the skirt—it didn't matter.

He twisted his wrist free and brought his hand to his mouth. He slid first his ring finger, then his middle between his lips, his eyes hot and lecherous.

The thumb of the hand still covering my lips slid across my cheek.

"Celine, darling, are you ready to be quiet now?"

I nodded eagerly under his hand.

"Good, because we're here."

It took my lust-addled mind a moment to comprehend his meaning, and when it did, I recognized that the carriage was no longer moving.

When had that happened? And how the devil was I going to show my face?

The hand on my lips disappeared, in its place a damp forefinger. Like the brazen hussy I was, I took it between my lips and swirled my tongue around the exact way he preferred when I was on my knees for him.

It was Gabriel's turn to bite back a groan. "Lord, I love you," he bit out, leaning back against the seat breathing heavy. With a little shuffle, he adjusted his breeches, drawing my gaze there and another whimper from my lips.

"Fuck…" he muttered to himself. "You had too much to drink, darling. That's why you're flushed and disheveled. Right?"

I nodded.

"Good," he said, then clambered out of the carriage. I heard him dismiss the driver and footman, before handing me out himself. On shaky legs I stepped out and paused before him.

He adjusted my cloak, settling it more fully on my shoulders. A brief glance down showed the extent of his efforts on my chest. Reddened with arousal and irritation from the morning's growth on his chin. I didn't even wish to know what the rest of me looked like.

His hand found mine, and he pulled me along behind him to the door where Reeves waited for us.

"How was your evening, my lord? My lady?" he asked properly, reaching for my cloak immediately.

I was only capable of a nod.

"Lady Rycliffe is feeling a little unwell, Reeves." He mimed drinking while he said it. Oh, I would punish him for that. "I'll see to her toilette tonight. You can send the rest of the staff to bed."

Reeves nodded, an entirely unconvinced expression on his face.

Rather than assisting me up the stairs, Gabriel picked me up. It was a struggle to stifle my surprised gasp when I found myself in his arms, one arm banding about my shoulder blades, the other under my knees. But I managed.

Gabriel dipped his head down, not pausing in his climb of the stairs. "I know what you're doing, darling," he breathed in my ear.

I merely raised a brow in response.

"You mean to punish me by withholding your sounds from me—now that you are free to make them without scandalizing the staff. Don't worry, I have ways of drawing them out."

He fumbled with the door to our room and me for a moment before setting me down to finish the task. We spilled into the room before he pressed me back against the wooden door. He spun the key in the lock with a decisive *click*.

My ardor had cooled slightly. His, apparently, had not. Gabriel's tongue worked against mine in the filthiest possible manner.

Dimly, I was aware of his hands working at the hooks lining my spine. But when the obstacle proved to be too much, he grabbed both edges and tugged. A few of the hooks gave way, and I broke from his lips to glare at him. He knew my thoughts on the destruction of my clothing, particularly my ball gowns.

Rather than offer the sheepish apology I was owed, he spun me around and undid the last of them before yanking the gown down to the floor. Petticoats met a similar—though less violent—fate. My stays loosened before I realized he had undone the knot, but the sound of him yanking the cord through the holes swirled with my harsh breaths.

Any lust that had been dampened with our trip into the house was rushing back through my veins.

He shoved my chemise down to join its sisters. A groan echoed along my spine before his lips found the left cheek of my buttock. A sharp nip followed before he spun me around and I stood bare before him, save for slippers and stockings.

A massive hand wrapped around my calf, lifting it to shove the layers of torn fabric out of the way before repeating the process with the other leg. Free of gown and underthings, he glided his hands up my thighs to settle on my hips.

On his knees before me, he eyed me with interest, his gaze lingering as he tried to decide where to tease me first. Eventually, he dropped a kiss on my low belly and in response I had to fight a whimper. Playfully, his tongue slid into my navel, swirling there and earning a giggle. One hand dropped down again, ghosting over my mound—too lightly—before finding my knee.

Gently, Gabriel urged me to lift my knee and pressed a kiss to it through my stocking. A fog of confusion descended before he guided my leg over his shoulder with a smug grin.

Oh my.

The hand on my hip slid forward, spreading me open for his perusal. That was all the warning I was to receive.

Gabriel fell on me, his tongue swirling through my folds in the way that never failed to take me apart. My head hinged back, hitting the door with an echoing *thunk*. I didn't care. I couldn't feel anything but his ministrations against my core, his soothing hand petting distractedly at my knee. And his hot breath against my nub.

One hand scrambled for purchase against the smooth wood behind me, the other tangled in his overgrown mahogany strands.

In my distraction, he almost pulled a moan from my chest. I took the hand flailing uselessly at the door and pressed it against my lips in a pale imitation of his efforts earlier.

His lips worked and his tongue swirled, and the hand at my knee slid up to my bottom. Without pausing his efforts to undo me, he raised the hand and brought it down on me.

A startled squeak escaped. And he pulled away, grinning.

"Told you," he murmured before returning to his efforts. It hadn't hurt, only startled me. The sting left behind was a pleasant sort, like when his teeth offered gentle nips along my skin.

He had won that war, so my hand abandoned my mouth and moved to join the other fisting in his hair. His hand abandoned my mound, catching mine. He dragged mine to take over the duty he had abandoned, spreading myself lasciviously for his feast.

Now free, he dipped two fingers in my channel, moving his lips and tongue to focus their efforts on my apex.

Whimpers, moans, and breathy pants of his name fell from my mouth, entirely unrestricted.

I was almost there. Desperately chasing my climax, hips canting against his face in a way that was almost certainly uncomfortable for him. He wouldn't care, he never did. And I was right. There.

One breathless whimper away from release when he pulled away. Lips and tongue abandoned my little button, and his fingers slid out from inside me. The only relief he offered was a palm pressed at my tiny peak.

A ragged sob broke from my chest, as I thrust against his hand, feeling my pleasure slip from me.

I knew. I *knew* it would be all the sweeter for our teasing game. But when he slipped my knee off his shoulder and rose before me, the heel of his hand still pressed unsatisfyingly against me, I was shocked to feel him brushing away tears with delicate—if sticky—fingers.

"Too much?" he asked against my throat.

Words were beyond me still. I nodded automatically before understanding his meaning and shaking my head.

The breath from his chuckle drifted along tight nipples earning him another whimper. "Which one, darling?"

The wave had receded enough to comprehend. "No, not too much." I broke off, swallowing harshly. "I can take more."

A massive hand cupped my cheek, drawing my gaze to his. "Of course you can. My girl can do anything... Except stay quiet."

I shoved weakly at his still-clothed chest.

"It is a very good thing that I love you to distraction. Otherwise, I could never abide your smug face."

"A very good thing," he agreed.

I slipped my hand down to palm his erection. He groaned, heavy and honeyed, before backing away.

"Not tonight. Tonight is for you," he insisted.

"But... Why?"

Our eyes met. Instead of the lust-blown pupils I expected, I found something tender, loving. He just shook his head, eyes slipping closed, before pressing a delicate kiss to my lips.

He pulled back, only enough for a breath to escape. "I'm feeling inspired," he said before dipping back down, lips slotting against mine in that perfect way of his.

Rather than pull away, his next words were pressed against my lips. "Let me, Cee? Let me love you the way I want? The way you deserve?"

"You already do," I insisted but let him guide me toward our bed. He took it upon himself to divest me of slippers and stockings. In retaliation, I tugged his loose cravat free before shoving his waistcoat off his shoulders.

Gabriel knew precisely what it did to me when he grabbed his shirt with one hand behind his neck and tugged it off. I wasn't entirely certain why I found the move so devastating, probably the way the muscles of his abdomen flexed with the effort.

One moment he was standing before me, the next he had me splayed beneath him on the silky bedcovers. Bergamot enveloped me. Gabriel was everything, everything I could see, smell, feel, taste. He was above me, beside me, and around me.

The impossibly adoring, tender warmth in his eye hadn't abandoned him. It was such a shift from the playfulness of before that I didn't know how to account for it.

Then his lips found mine, and I didn't particularly care for the explanation. An explanation would distract from this—this devastating way he poured himself into the kiss.

I thought I knew every single one of Gabriel's kisses by now. Hello, goodbye, you just did something I found particularly endearing, I'd like you to be wearing less clothing, I'm grateful you're wearing less clothing—I knew them all. But this kiss was different.

It brought memories of our first—on that veranda. But there was a different kind of desperation. He was a riptide, and I couldn't fight him. I would never survive the swim against his current.

Between his drugging kisses and his earlier efforts to wreck me, I was swept away, lost in sensation.

Arousal was licking at my skin once again. His every touch burned in the *best* possible way. And when he reached between us to bring us together in this final way, the connection took my breath away.

His lips broke from mine on a gasp, his forehead finding my collarbone with a curse.

And then he moved. He moved and I died. Just a little. Just for a moment. When I returned to my body, I was clutching at his side desperately, fingernails scoring along his back, frantically fisting a hand in his hair—trying to pull his lips back to mine. I needed his kiss more than air—air wasn't Gabriel, and I didn't need anything in the world that wasn't him and this moment.

Harsh, panted words slipped into my consciousness.

"—love you so damn much... Best thing that ever happened to me... Look at you and I can't breathe, you're so beautiful... Want to stay right here, just like this, forever..."

It took longer to register the sentiments and pleas escaping my own lips unbidden. Demands for more, for forever.

I was so close to the peak when he entered me that when the tide pulled me under, I drowned in him. Minutes, hours, days—the pleasure never ceased, knocking breath from my lungs and thought from my head.

I sensed Gabriel's shudder above me before his warm weight collapsed atop me, prolonging the trembling, gasping, drugging pleasure impossibly longer.

Eventually, he found the strength to roll to his side, pulling me with him. That was good. I wasn't ready to not be touching him.

Lazy fingers slipped through my bedraggled waves, undoing the occasional knot, but mostly just soothing away the occasional shudder.

"Gabriel?"

"Hmm?"

"What *was* that?"

He was silent for a moment. "Loving you..."

"But—"

"It was just one of the ways I love you, Cee."

I wrapped my arm tighter around his side. "Today was wonderful. We should do this every day."

His chuckle had shifted back to his usual honeyed tone. "Every day, forever."

"So, tomorrow, then?" I asked, shifting away just enough to meet warm, dark eyes.

"And the next day," he assured me. "Now, if I'm to have the strength to keep up with you, we need rest. Go to sleep."

"I love you," I murmured, tucking into his warmth.

I was half asleep when his reply came. "I love you too. So much." If anything came after, I would never know.

I drifted off in Gabriel's arms, in the most perfect heaven ever to exist.

Twenty

RYCLIFFE PLACE, LONDON - MAY 14, 1809

I AWOKE IN HELL.

Alone.

One moment, I was safe and warm and blissfully ignorant in sleep. Sated, content, heavenly in our bed.

Then a hysterical, piercing shriek rang from the street below.

I raced down the stairs, barefoot with my dressing gown half on. Crimson footprints led through the entry and down the hall by the time I reached the landing.

There had only been a minute—perhaps less—between the scream and my arrival on the scene. The front door banged against the outer railing in the breeze. Framed in the doorway, scarlet blood pooled on the stone steps. It glistened, reflecting the dawning light. Beside it, a bouquet of irises lay scattered and ragged. The petals stuck to the viscous red puddle as they blew over the top.

Alone in the entry, I was left with no other choice but to follow the trail in a numb kind of revulsion. I slipped, my bare feet offering little purchase against the sticky trails on the marble. I managed to catch myself against the wall just inside the dining room.

The eerie silence of the hall had descended into cacophonous chaos there.

A maid crashed into me in her haste to get... somewhere.

In an effort to remove myself from the turmoil, I backed into someone else. At last, one of the footmen took pity on me. Firmly, he pressed me back against the open door with orders to stay put.

Someone brushed past. Someone else moved aside. The stars aligned and I caught my first view of the table. Of him.

There was no surprise. I heard the scream, and I knew. My husband. My Gabriel.

He lay face up on the table, his brow furrowed with pain, sweat pooling at his temples.

I could not see the wound from my vantage—too many people between us—but the blood....

So much blood.

The world narrowed to a pinhole. There was only my husband's pained face

I hadn't felt him leave. That insipid, ridiculous, meaningless thought refused to leave my mind as my husband bled on our dining-room table. It swirled and formed and reformed and refused to abate.

The servants brushing past, obscuring my view were an annoyance. Their chatter was little more than a senseless buzz. Nothing made sense. Nothing was discernible. Not until the groan.

Gabriel's pained moan of my name... I had the utterly inane thought that it did not sound so terribly different from the sounds he made during pleasure. But his voice, my name, and only those were enough to jolt me from my frozen position. To close the distance.

How many minutes had I wasted fixed to that door? Two? Three? How many did we have left?

Not enough. Never enough.

My hand found his, tacky in my own. Now at his side I saw the extent of the damage. I did not have to be a surgeon to know...

He tried to rise, to look at his abdomen. With my free hand I brushed his hair back, urging him down gently.

I shuffled closer, hovering over him. "Stay still," I whispered.

"Cee..."

"Shh, I'm here." His grip tightened weakly in response.

"Cee—" A pained grunt broke through whatever he meant to say when one of the servants pressed against his abdomen. "Everyone out," he hissed through gritted teeth.

"But sir..." someone protested.

"I want to be alone with my wife."

He knew too.

I couldn't breathe.

If I breathed, the tears would come. And I had to be able to see.

One by one they filed out, abandoning bloody rags and bowls filled with water that was surely clear at one time. The last closed the door behind them with a decisive click.

"Celine, darling, you need to breathe," he choked out.

I shook my head. Words weren't going to come without tears.

"Can't have you fainting. Need to see those pretty green eyes."

Acquiescing, my inhale was ragged and the exhale more so. He raised one hand, cupping my cheek before letting it fall back to his side.

"I always thought I would know what to say when it happened. That was rather overconfident of me."

I nodded, not really comprehending him.

"One of the reasons you love me," he added.

"Of many," I agreed. The words broke free from deep in my chest.

"Celine, I've never been accused of being a good man. But loving you... it's the best thing I've ever done."

The sob burst forth without permission, tears obscuring my vision as I feared. I was left with no choice but to bury my face in his chest, and his free hand found the back of my head.

"Shh..."

"I'm supposed to be comforting you," I protested.

"You are. It hardly hurts at all anymore."

No! Not enough time!

I pressed myself back up to look at him. This time when I tightened my grip on his hand, there was no answering tug.

I understood then, what he meant about not knowing what to say. How do you choose from the hundreds, thousands, millions of sentiments and declarations and promises? And every ragged wordless breath was a waste of precious seconds we didn't have.

"Gabriel..." It was more sob than word, but he seemed to understand.

"It's all right. I already know."

"But..."

"You told me... every single moment... of every single day." My tears were mixing with his own, pooling on his chest. Each of his breaths came shallower than the last, each blink longer than the one before.

And then the words came to me.

"Close your eyes," I breathed.

"You going to kiss me this time too?"

At my nod, he did. And I did, pressing my trembling lips against his unnaturally cool ones. He pressed back before they went still beneath mine.

I knew his eyes wouldn't open again. I rested my head on his chest while my tears soaked the parts of his shirt not already sticky with blood.

And I listened to his heartbeats, every last one.

Twenty-One

RYCLIFFE PLACE, LONDON - MAY 14, 1809

IF I KNELT THERE, my head pressed to his chest long after the last beat of his heart, just to be certain, there was no one to judge. If minutes turned to an hour turned to two and the warmth left him, that was my right.

I didn't have enough time before. I would take it now. Because as soon as I rose from the sticky puddle pooling about my knees, after would begin and no amount of time would be enough for me to be ready for after.

In the end it was Jane who turned my now into after. She was the one who tugged me from Gabriel's side to wash and dress and ask questions I could neither hear nor answer. I hated her for that. I did not want his blood off of me. I wanted his arms around me.

I wanted none of this to be happening.

Clean and pressed, she brought me down the back stairwell. The entry must still be in a state. Eventually, they propped me on a settee in the drawing room like some sort of posable doll. Mrs. Talbot came with food and drink, as if anything I consumed would stay down.

Reeves came next, with questions of how to word a note to the duke and duchess.

His mother.

That thought, more than any other, shattered the paralyzed impotence that had settled over me.

"I will go," I said.

"But, my lady, you are not fit to visit anyone," Reeves protested.

"Not a note."

"I beg your pardon?"

"You will not tell Her Grace that her son is gone in a note. I will go."

"Very well. I will have the carriage readied."

"I will walk."

"You will…"

"Walk. Yes."

Reeves, clearly at a loss with me, merely sighed. I should be kinder to him. His day had been truly terrible as well.

After a brief conference with Jane with a fair amount of back and forth, she returned with the only plain bonnet I had and a dark spencer. Apparently I was supposed to arrive at Hasket House dressed as death itself. As if my countenance alone would not be sufficient to convey the somber tone of my visit.

After I put a stop to another discussion on the merits of traveling with a footman, the staff decided to leave me to my own devices.

I was ushered out the back door, but a glance at the front step told me what I already knew. Cleaned away. The only remnant of the morning's horror was a single brown stain.

I ducked my head, hiding under my bonnet in a desperate hope that I would not meet with anyone I knew. In this, at least, I was lucky. However, in my distraction I made a wrong turn.

I did not notice. Not when I knocked on the door. Not when I saw the butler. Not when the entry was filled with rich sages and golds instead of stark blacks and whites. Not until I heard her voice behind me.

"Celine?"

That was all it took.

"Mama..." I collapsed into her, and her arms held me easily, fiercely as I broke.

Dimly, I felt her shooing servants away. I pressed my face tighter into her shoulder. She loosened one hand to untie my crushed bonnet, letting it fall to the floor. Her arms returned to my shoulders, tighter even than before.

Every ragged sob I had managed to restrain this morning came free in great desperate gasps. "I cannot breathe."

I did not know how she possibly understood my words, but she replied, "Hush. I know, *cherie*. I know."

I had no idea how long I stood in the entryway of Mama's house, sobbing in her arms. But never once did her grip loosen. At some point I became aware that my own shoulder was damp, and the implications of that began to dawn.

I pulled away and her face was as tearstained as my own surely was. She brushed my cheeks with thumbs in a futile effort and pressed a kiss to my forehead. My sobs had quieted, leaving only silent tears behind for the moment. She pulled me into the drawing room, to the settee, and drew the curtains before sitting beside me.

"He's gone." My voice was hollow, brittle, and entirely foreign, just like the words themselves.

She took a deep, shuddering breath before pressing another kiss to my forehead. "I know," she said, cupping my cheek and brushing a few more tears.

"How?"

"I remember when it was me. When every breath was a

knife to my chest. I am so sorry, *cherie*. If I could fix this... If I could bear this for you, I would."

"I don't know how to do this."

"I know," she replied with a thick swallow. "I never prepared you for this. I hoped you would never experience it. To be honest, I wouldn't have known how to prepare you for it, even if I'd tried."

"How did you? When Papa and..."

"I have no idea." Her answer was an odd little half laugh through tears. "One moment at a time, I suppose."

"I just stood there. I didn't do anything until he called for me. I wasted so much time."

"Celine, there was nothing you could have done. And there never would have been enough time."

"You don't even know how he..."

"But I know you. If love and will alone could have kept his soul in his body, you would have done it. And I know how he loved you. He would not have left you if there were any other way."

With a tremulous breath, I laid my head in her lap, shuddering as she ran her fingers through my hair.

"I was supposed to go to Hasket House... They wanted to send a note, but I couldn't. Not in a note."

"It will make no difference if they learn now or an hour from now. We'll go when you're ready."

"You will come too?"

"Try to stop me."

"*Je t'aime, Mama.*"

"*Moi aussi. Toujours.*"

~

I REMEMBERED LITTLE from telling the duke and duchess of their loss.

The days that followed were a blur of detached meetings and occasional moments of horrifying clarity. When Jane first held out a black crepe dress instead of lavender silk. The first time I was termed a widow. The first time Gabriel was named my late husband. Funeral arrangements. The first—and last—meal served on the dining-room table where my husband drew his final breath. The first time I slipped out of the servants' entrance, unable to bear the sight of the stain.

Each moment was its own kind of torture. And each one was perhaps a bit less painful than the last.

My pain was not lessening, of course, I had simply become accustomed to the unbearable agony that was each breath, and the one after, and all the breaths to come.

A modest attempt was made to find my husband's murderer, but the pursuit was abandoned long before I was satisfied with their efforts.

Weeks became months, then a year. Full mourning became half mourning, then everyday dress. The rest of the *ton* moved on. And I developed a peculiar sort of habit in my solitude.

"*Bonjour, mon amor*," I whispered, brushing my hand along the cold damp of my husband's headstone.

Some days, like today, the ground outside Hasket House was clammy, and I sat on the bench I'd had moved closer. Other days I brought a blanket and sat beside him.

"I practiced my quarte perry this morning. I'm getting quite good, if I do say so myself. Davina and Xander were in fine form the other day. I believe he took the last of the tarts, and she may never forgive him for it. What else? Oh, your mother is hosting a ball next month. I think I will have to send my regrets for this one. Perhaps the next one.

"Marie has invited me to join her on a visit to a new gaming hell next week. It promises to be entirely inappropriate fun. I suspect you would never forgive me if I rejected her offer. I hope you will help me at the tables. I should hate to disappoint you by losing..."

The End and the Beginning

HASKET HOUSE, LONDON - JUNE 5, 1816

IT WAS A RITUAL NOW, pressing a kiss to my fingertips before dropping it to him. Spreading the blanket above him and settling down, my back against his cool, broad form. On days such as this, he was a balm against the oppressive, damp summer heat.

"Bonjour, mon amor. Et joyeux anniversaire."

I allowed myself a moment for the grief to come. It was always particularly sharp on these kinds of days. It had once been an open wound, gaping and bleeding. Then it burned with fever and infection. Now, it was an old, familiar pain. Some days it was a dull ache, easily ignored. Others, like today, it throbbed in reminder, but it was manageable.

More and more frequently, the pain was shrouded in guilt. It should not be so easily biddable. At one time, I could not open my eyes without thoughts of him. Last week I made it until luncheon before a bite of cheese reminded me of his teasing expression. That my earlier greeting was hindered only by a lump in my throat instead of the all-encompassing sobs of years past—that was perhaps the greater hurt.

It was a nonsensical thought. My husband had been gone

for seven years. I had been talking to his headstone for four times longer than we had been married. A lone tear escaped, and I brushed it away.

My sorrow was quiet this year.

Gabriel had not been a good man, not by anyone's definition, but he had been good to me, loved me. He would not wish my wraithlike existence of the first few years to continue.

With that hopeful thought, I continued with my ritual. "I don't suppose you know what one wears to a masquerade held in a gaming hell. A masquerade hosted by the wife of one's former lover, even." The only response was a light breeze brushing through my curls.

"I thought not. Perhaps the deep plum with the beads? It's a bit outdated, but there's a certain theatricality to it that might suit for a masquerade." The fluff of a dandelion danced across the tip of my foot on its journey to somewhere new.

"I'm glad we're in agreement. Your mother is planning to wear something in the style of Marie Antionette. For all I know, it's one of the woman's actual gowns. You know your mother would not consider it to be overdone." A great tit landed on the nearby oak branch, chirping its usual two syllables at me.

"I do not know what your sister will wear. Perhaps something she stole from that pirate captain your brother and I had to barter her return from last month. She is determined to vex him into an early grave. Are we certain she is not in line to inherit?"

A cloud shifted and the sun found my face, bathing it in a pleasant warmth. Somehow this warmth was peaceful instead of muggy as it had been earlier.

"Michael told me that Lord Champaign may be in attendance tonight. No one has seen him in some years, and it's all very mysterious. You know how I love a mysterious man....

Perhaps he will favor me with a dance. I know how you appreciated his attentions toward me before we wed."

The breeze picked up slightly, clouds returning to veil the sun and the oak leaves rustling their discontent at the disturbance.

"I wish you could come with me. Can you imagine the fun we would have had at a masquerade? And at a gaming hell? The *ton* never would have recovered from our mischief. There are a great many darkened corners in Wayland's. You wouldn't have been able to resist dragging me to one and having your way with me. I would have let you think you were the seducer, but in that plum gown, I would have seduced you."

One of the irises I had planted around his resting place brushed against my arm as the pale-blue butterfly inspecting it moved on to the next.

I was not delusional. My husband was dead. I knew these events were the happenstances of nature and nothing more. That breezes and butterflies happened every day all across the country. I knew they happened around me without notice. A regular, uneventful coincidence when I promenaded through the park or stepped into the carriage.

But here, in the little Hasket family plot, they felt different, special.

They were an enticing awareness down my spine.

They were Gabriel.

The End

The Most Imprudent Matches series and Celine's story will continue in *Angel of Mine*.

Support the author. Leave a review on Amazon!

Acknowledgments

Thank you to *all* my friends and family for your support in this and all my projects.

Thank you to my mother for all of the things.

Thank you to Martha limiting the amount of times you say "I told you so."

Thank you, as always, to Bryton for dragging me out of the house on occasion.

Thank you to Mariah for your unending support.

Thank you to Laura Linn for becoming my friend over our willingness to devastate our readers.

Thank you Holly Perret at The Swoonies Romance Art for my breathtaking cover.

About the Author

Ally Hudson was raised in Hudson, Ohio. Currently, she resides in Fort Wayne, Indiana, with a very sassy dog. *Devil of Mine* is a prequel novella in the Most Imprudent Matches series. She writes of cinnamon-bun heroes, snarky friendships, and true love. Her other hobbies include reading, embroidery, and re-watching television shows she has seen ten times already.